UNDERGROUNDERS

DAVID SKUY

Scholastic Canada Ltd.

Toronto New York London Auckland Sydney
Mexico City New Delhi Hong Kong Buenos Aires

Scholastic Canada Ltd.
604 King Street West, Toronto, Ontario M5V 1E1, Canada
Scholastic Inc.
557 Broadway, New York, NY 10012, USA
Scholastic Australia Pty Limited
PO Box 579, Gosford, NSW 2250, Australia
Scholastic New Zealand Limited
Private Bag 94407, Botany, Manukau 2163, New Zealand
Scholastic Children's Books
Euston House, 24 Eversholt Street, London NW1 1DB, UK

Library and Archives Canada Cataloguing in Publication
Skuy, David, 1963-
        Undergrounders / David Skuy.
ISBN 978-1-4431-0728-0
        I. Title.
PS8637.K88U64 2011   jC813'.6   C2010-906031-8

    6 5 4 3 2 1   Printed in Canada 121 11 12 13 14 15

To Mom.

Chapter 1

BANG! BANG! BANG!

The noise scared me at first, until I turned around and saw this kid in a dark-blue hockey jersey and a black tuque staring at me through the wire mesh that went around the hockey rink. The kid was banging away on the boards with his stick. I was about to flip him the finger and take off when he called out to me, "You mind getting our puck?" He nodded to the kid next to him. "This loser doesn't know how to shoot."

The other kid was real big and wore the same hockey jersey. "It's not easy to deflect a puck off the crossbar and over the fence. That's true talent," the big kid said, laughing.

"Give me a break," the first kid said. "You couldn't do that again if you took a million shots."

I really don't know why I helped. I really don't. I was freezing cold and totally hungry. All I'd eaten today was a bag of chips. Why should I care about a couple of Reggies? That's what Undergrounders call kids with regular lives, kids who go to school and have parents — and play hockey — and who don't live on the streets. Of course, I didn't exactly live on the streets. I lived in the Underground with Lewis and Rigger and all the other Undergrounders.

"It's over by that blue van, I think," the first kid said. "Could you look? We got our skates on and can't go on the pavement."

I shoved my hands into my pockets. Some idiot had stolen my gloves last night; my hands were about to come off. Lewis said it's the cold that'll kill you, not the streets. I think not eating is the killer, but I didn't say anything because he was a lot older and didn't like it when I didn't agree.

I found the puck leaning against one of the blue van's tires, and the two Reggies cheered when they saw I'd got it.

"Toss it over the fence. Thanks a lot. We owe you one," the first kid said.

A third player came over. He wore the same jersey as the other two. I figured they must be on the same hockey team.

"Did you get it, or what?" the third kid demanded. He sounded real angry. "I'm freezing standing around."

"We got it. We got it," the big kid said. "Chill out."

"That's the problem," the angry kid said. "I am chilled out."

I threw the puck as far as I could onto the ice. It felt good to move my arms like that. Two of them chased after it. The first kid banged his stick on the boards.

"Thanks again. If you live around here you should

come play. We're here after school most days." He turned to join the shinny game. I don't meet many friendly guys like that.

Weird how I hated hockey now. I used to love it. I was on a real team, and was always playing street hockey and at school. For some reason the sight of these guys playing hockey made my chest feel heavy. The grumbling in my stomach was all the motivation I needed to leave, anyway. I had to eat soon or I'd faint.

I tried to remember when I had last played. For sure it was way before my mom died, maybe just before we moved to Brentwood after my mom lost her job at the auto parts factory. I usually forced myself not to think of my mom because it made me too sad. Once I cried about her a bit and one of the Undergrounders, Will, made fun of me and everyone was laughing and calling me a big baby and stuff. Now that I was all alone I let myself remember a bit. Ron had got a part-time job in Brentwood, so off we went. I most definitely didn't like thinking of that jerk, and I'll never know why my mom made him her boyfriend. She said she was lonely after Dad left, and Ron made her laugh. He never made me laugh, not once.

I was in the hospital room when Mom begged Ron to take care of me after she died because there was no one else. The doctors had told her the cancer was too big in her body. I was crying and Ron said, "No problem, Angela." I heard him say it.

"Be strong, my sweet boy. It'll be okay, I promise. Ron will take care of things. It'll be fine. You're a strong boy —

and so smart. Things will be good. I know you're sad, and so am I. Just remember that your mommy loves you — I'll love you forever, for all time. Just remember I'll be keeping my eye on you from heaven, so make me proud. Just remember you'll always be my angel boy."

Those were the last words she ever said to anyone. She fell asleep and never woke up. Never even opened her eyes. The cancer plain killed her. Even though I knew she had only died a bit more than a year ago, it sometimes seemed like a million years — and then sometimes it felt like only yesterday.

Ron was a liar, that's for sure, because he disappeared the day after my mom died, ran off just like my dad. I woke up that morning and he was gone. I made some toast, although the bread was totally old and gross. Then someone started pounding on the door. I figured it was Ron and I yelled, "The door's open, idiot!" The pounding kept going so I opened it and there was the landlord all red in the face and with angry eyes.

"I knew you were no good!" he yelled. "It was stupid for me to rent to losers."

I didn't care what he said about Ron, but there was no way he could say that about my mom.

"My mom's not a loser. *You* are — you stupid jerk," and I gave him my best glare.

He sort of caught me off guard by grabbing me by the collar and pulling me outside. I struggled but he was strong for an old guy. "Don't sass me. I'm out three months' rent because I felt sorry for your mom. I just

4

saw Ron drive off with his car packed, which makes me doubt he'll ever pay me, and I sure don't think you got the money."

He let go of my collar and looked at me real hard. I had no idea how much three months' rent was, but I knew I didn't have it. All I had was five bucks in quarters and loonies, and a ten-dollar bill I'd found under the couch back a few months, which fell out of Ron's pocket when he was sleeping.

"Ron cleared out. Now you have to clear out in ten minutes or I'm calling the cops. Ten minutes or you're going to jail!" he thundered.

"But my mom . . ." I stammered.

That softened him up a bit. He shrugged and said, "Okay. Maybe you can take the morning to call your relatives, pack up and go. But I need you out by twelve. I have to clean this place up and show it to possible renters tomorrow morning." And then he was gone.

My mom had no family. Ron was supposed to take care of me. I never knew my dad. He took off before I was born. "Nothin' wrong with being a single mom," she always said to me. "You're the only man I need since I love you so much." I knew she loved me, but for some reason she let Ron stay with us, and look where that got me. I guess love doesn't make you smart. So I was on my own, and I wasn't going to wait for the police. I grabbed my sleeping bag from under my bed. I got it when I was a little kid, and it wasn't much thicker than a towel, but I figured it was better than nothing. Then I stuffed some clothes into a knapsack, and with only a small picture of my mom, left that bogus apartment and never looked back. Been on the streets since then.

At first it wasn't so bad. In the summer I could sleep in the forest down by the river, only it kept getting colder and I think I might have frozen to death if Lewis hadn't got me into the Underground. He saved my life and was my best friend, which is why I didn't mind doing business stuff for him like delivering packages.

The Underground was an old abandoned part of a building behind the train station. Some crazy guy started to build a shopping mall, but he never built more than the underground part. Lewis said he ran out of money. An older kid, called Rigger because his last name was Riggins — and he wasn't really a kid but more like an adult — figured out how to get water from a pipe with no one finding out. Rigger charged fifty cents a night to sleep there, but it was worth it. We Undergrounders were different from Streeters because we had a place to sleep at night.

I left Cedarview Park and the outdoor rink and kept walking about twenty minutes until I got to the alley, which was a sweet shortcut Lewis showed me to get to the Market. I wanted to hawk at least two bucks today, and I had to get a good spot near the front doors. Then I'd have enough to give to Rigger for rent tonight, and have extra for some Chinese buns and maybe even a drink. Yesterday, I was late and had to go to the back of the Market, and there was hardly any traffic, or maybe all the cheapskates came out that door on account of street kids bugging them for money all the time.

I would have loved to be in the Underground right now. Rigger was strict about that and we had to clear out in the morning by nine and couldn't come back until after five, which was hours from now. I would turn into a Popsicle by then. Stupid weather. I jingled the two quarters together in my pocket. Enough to pay rent for tonight, but nothing for eating, and my stomach was like a black hole pulling at me, like an itch you can't scratch.

Chapter 2

The backs of the stores lined one side of the alley, with garages on the other. The recycling bins and stuff lined up against the garages made it a pain to walk on that side so I scrunched over against the stores to get out of that stupid wind that was freezing my face off. I was thinking about the Market and where to hawk when I saw a screen door at the bottom of some stairs that was open a crack.

Double quick I hopped down the stairs and slid in between the screen and the door to the building as best I could. It felt so good to get out of the wind for a few minutes. I hunkered down and wrapped my hands around me and under my armpits. My feet were cold but at least it was a bit warmer in here. Only it was boring all crunched up behind a door, and soon I decided to leave. I pulled myself up by the door handle — and guess what? It turned! I kept turning it, and pushed a bit with my shoulder, and the door actually opened.

The warm rolled over me like a wave when you're floating in the ocean. I went to the ocean with my mom and Ron once; at least they said it was the ocean but I knew it was actually a lake. Still, it was big, and even though it wasn't salty it was fun. A crazy idea hit me. It was Sunday morning and stores probably weren't open yet. I could sneak inside for a few minutes and warm up for real.

I was too cold to care anyway and was inside before I knew it, although I closed the door too loud and gave myself a total heart attack. I tucked myself into a corner behind some boxes and made myself real small. That wasn't hard to do for me — I wasn't the biggest kid in the world. Lewis called me Mouse, and I didn't mind when he did it, but then all the Undergrounders started calling me that, and it bugged me but I couldn't do anything about it. I would have killed to get bigger.

Slowly, my eyes adjusted to the darkness. There were boxes all over the place, and piles of sweaters, hockey pants and other equipment. I knew where I was — in the basement of Baxter's, a hockey store. I think they sold other stuff too, but mostly it was hockey. I passed it all the time on the way to the Market when I didn't take the alley. Best part was I knew it was closed on Sundays.

It was dead quiet. The place had to be empty. No reason to stay curled up in a little ball, so I started to wander a bit. Rows of skates rested on wooden shelves, and the other equipment was organized into sections: pants, shin pads, elbow pads, helmets. I could tell it was used stuff.

Bang!

I dropped to the floor in a panic and looked around real frantic. I'm dead, I thought. Lewis had told me about kid jail — he called it juvie, which is short for juvenile detention. It's where the cops put kids who are criminals. He'd been there when he was fourteen and he said it's the worst place in the world — vicious guards and other kids pounding you, and no food, and work all the time.

Bang!

Then I had to laugh. The noise was the screen door blowing in the wind. What a doofus move to leave it open. I went back out and closed it tight, then tiptoed over to the stairs leading to the main floor. Keeping real low, I crept up and poked my head over the top step, feeling kind of like those woodchucks that I saw in a movie at school about nature. Me and James, who was my best friend, fired spitballs at Sophie Kelly until our teacher caught us. Boy, did we get in trouble.

Racks of hockey sticks blocked the window to the street, so I figured it was safe to check things out. At the back of the store they'd hung all the new skates on the wall like trophies. The skates were shiny, and the prices almost took my breath away. One pair cost $750. I could live forever on that kind of coin. Farther along a large sign read *Junior Section*. One pair was totally sick — Grafs — blacker than the rest with a silver line running along the sole. Even the blade was shiny. I took it down — light as a feather. I turned the price tag around so I could see it — $525. Unbelievable!

I knew it was wrong. I knew it was crazed. But I just

had to have them. I tried to resist — I did — and even picked through some jerseys. But no chance. The idea of skating on that rink was too strong. There were tons of skate boxes lined up against the wall. They wouldn't even notice one missing. It didn't take me too long to find the Grafs. I tried on a nine and it was huge. The eight was also big, so I took a seven and figured that would work. I was so freaked at what I was doing I thought my heart was going to explode.

I had already spotted this awesome Easton stick so I grabbed that, and then I saw hockey gloves hung on pegs near the front window. How great would new gloves be? I became like a total criminal and snagged a pair of red and blue ones. Then I saw this bin of winter mitts, and I needed those. Lucky they had some black bags with shoulder straps, and I stuffed all that junk into the bag. I knew I'd been here too long; time to make tracks, as Lewis said, before the cops came. Only I remembered I'd need a puck and stuffed one into the bag, along with a roll of stick tape, and finally a blue Maple Leafs hockey sweater.

But that's not the worst thing I did. I nosed around the cash register and found a box with some money in it — a five-dollar bill. Jackpot! And to top it off, in the fridge there was this huge submarine sandwich and a can of Coke, and guess where that ended up!

I know stealing is wrong. My mom taught me that. My mom said she'd be looking down on me from heaven, which made me feel good usually. I prayed she was too busy right now to be watching. She sure wouldn't be happy with me. But somehow I couldn't stop myself.

In no time I was outside and tearing down the alley as fast as I could. Even though I'm small, I'm fast. I stopped after I got back to the street and scarfed that sandwich, and the Coke disappeared in seconds. I had to keep reminding myself that this wasn't a dream, that this was really happening. I had money, skates, a stick, gloves; I wasn't even cold anymore. I hadn't been warm, I mean really warm, in I don't know how long.

I was beyond stoked when I thought about the skates. Instead of wandering the streets all day with nothing to do, I could go to the rink and skate and shoot the puck around.

So maybe I didn't really hate hockey.

Chapter 3

I went right back to the rink. If those boys were gone I was going to try these skates out, even if they weren't sharpened. No chance I was going out with them there. I hadn't played hockey in over a year, and I knew I'd completely suck. I walked across the parking lot and looked over the boards. It was all mine! The change room was off to the side of the rink, so I went in and sat in the corner.

Next second I couldn't believe how dumb I'd been. Lewis said a street kid's got to be on the lookout for trouble because it comes out of nowhere, and he was right. Those kids came back. They must have just finished playing and gone to the vending machines. I recognized the three kids who'd asked me for the puck.

"I'm gonna bomb out in Math tomorrow," the big kid said. "Every time I tried to study I fell asleep."

"That's because you only tried once and then went to bed," the friendly kid laughed.

The big kid didn't get angry. "I'll just sneak into the gifted class and cheat off your sister."

"She'll kick your butt if you try — but go for it."

They punched fists. Obviously they were buds like me and Lewis. That big kid was really huge, almost as big as Lewis — and Lewis was sixteen. These kids didn't look older than me.

"You free tomorrow, Rasheed?" the angry kid asked the friendly kid.

"Yeah. We practise on Tuesday, so we can play here tomorrow after school." He tugged on the big kid's shirt. "Collin, you in?"

"Like I'm gonna miss a chance to dangle you? Of course I'm in."

"Awesome. Derrick?" Rasheed asked the angry kid.

"Sounds good," Derrick answered.

"So is everyone in?" Rasheed asked, and they all nodded.

I was putting on my skates the entire time, keeping my head down so they wouldn't notice me. Lewis had warned me about getting too close to Reggies. Said they'll turn on you and pound you something bad. I'd finished lacing up one skate when I noticed things got darker. I looked up. Rasheed was in front of me.

"Sorry. We just finished playing like five minutes ago. But we're coming tomorrow after school. You should come out."

Of course I couldn't play with these guys, but he wasn't moving, so I had to say something.

"Don't think I can do it tomorrow. Got stuff goin' on . . . tomorrow. Maybe."

Rasheed shrugged. "Come out if you can. We could always use another skater."

I assumed that was that, and began tying my other skate.

"Where do you go to school? I've never seen you around."

Street kids learn to think quick. I was ready. "I'm not from around here. My family's visiting my uncle. Got so boring I had to escape."

Rasheed bought it. Lewis always said that Reggies believe anything.

"Awesome-looking skates," he said. "Did you get them for Christmas?"

They obviously looked new. I pretended he'd figured it out. "Got new gloves too." I held them up.

"Sweet gloves. Wish I had new ones." He held his up — they were kind of old and beat-up.

"Come on, Rasheed. We're going to Derrick's."

"I'm coming." He nodded to me. "See you later. Our hockey team practises Tuesdays or Thursdays, and games are usually Friday or Saturday, and we're here most other times."

"Yeah . . . okay . . . maybe . . ."

That sounded so lame. Rasheed didn't say anything mean, though. "Thanks for getting our puck," was all, and as he left he called out, "That was our last one."

It was strange how nervous I got around Reggies. I put it out of my mind and hit the ice. I didn't do too badly, either, considering I hadn't skated in so long and the skates weren't sharpened. It might sound like bragging, but I was the star player on my team. When my mom still had a good job I played AA. I was a centre and scored a ton of goals. She couldn't afford for me to play competitive last year, and then she got sick.

The skating came right back to me. Before long I was whizzing around. Then I got my stick and puck. It was rough at first. The puck wouldn't behave and my stick was a bit long. I did okay after a while. Besides, this was better than hawking at the Market any day.

I don't really know how long I skated — a few hours definitely. I could have kept going but my hands and feet were becoming ice blocks again. I blasted one more slapshot at the net.

Clang!

It pinged off the post — the sickest sound in the world. More fun hitting the post than scoring sometimes. Nice way to end it, I thought, and collected the puck and went in. The change room was empty. As soon as I sat down I got hungry again. The vending machines were torturing me because I didn't have enough change. Usually, I ate a Chinese bun for dinner, but not tonight. I was going to get me a hot dog from the vendor in front of the train station.

"You need something for blisters."

A man in a dark-green shirt and dirty overalls pointed at my feet. I noticed two huge blisters on the outside part of my feet.

"You should not skate so long. Bad for feet."

His English wasn't the best, but he was right about the blisters. They looked nasty.

16

"No big deal," I said. "The skates are new. I gotta break them in better. Thanks."

He shook his head, peering at me funny. His face was baggy and had little bumps and marks all over it, and he had a thin scar over one of his eyes. "Not good skates," he muttered, and left.

I figured he was the janitor or something. I ignored him and tossed my stuff into my bag. I was about to leave when he came back.

"Here." He pushed a load of Band-Aids into my hand. "Use to make better."

The blisters were stinging a bit. "Thanks," I said, and put a couple on. He nodded and said, "My name Pavel. You ask if you need something."

I needed tons of stuff. Pavel hardly seemed the type to give it to me. He didn't look much better off than a Streeter himself. We talked a little and I found out he worked for the city as a janitor, going around to different rinks and community centres to clean up.

I said goodbye and hustled to the Market to see if I could hawk a bit of cash. On the way I stashed my stuff in my secret hiding spot behind the Theatre. There were these two huge metal garbage bins, and behind them were two window wells. Lewis had told me ages ago to find a secret hiding spot, and this was mine. I used it all the time and had never lost anything.

I wasn't surprised to see the front door of the Market crawling with Streeters and Undergrounders. We had rules about crowding. Once you set up, no one could come within five metres without permission.

Skidder had the front door, with Happy D and Fitzy. They were big kids and would never let me in. Creeper was at the side doors. He sometimes cut me some slack, so I went over with as friendly a smile as I could make. His face was kind of angry, maybe because of the cold. But then he was usually in a bad mood.

"What's up, Creeper? How's the money flow?"

"It sucks big time," he snarled back. "I ain't got no time for you, Mouse. Get scarce."

That didn't go well. Once Creeper got like that there was no point trying to be nice. My last chance was the passage to the parking lot in the back. It was the worst spot. Lewis had told me that. People hate feeling bad about themselves and street kids depress them. They feel guilty about how much money they have, and especially guilty when they won't give it to street kids. They feel real bad carrying bags of food from the Market, and the farther they walk away from the Market the worse they feel. So if you beg by the parking lot, you'll have a killer time trying to get a slimy cent out of them.

I wasn't too worried because of the five bucks in my pocket, and my hands and feet were freezing again. The Market was definitely slow today because after like twenty minutes maybe ten people walked by me, and they didn't so much as turn to look my way.

A mom with two small kids headed toward me, the kids so bundled in snowsuits all I could see were their tiny noses sticking out. Moms almost never give to street kids, and absolutely never when they had little kids with them. Best target is a guy with a lady; the guy will want to show off.

One of the kids pulled on his mom's coat.

In a whisper I heard the mom say, "Joshua, it's freezing and we're late. I can't stop every time."

"Give me a quarter, Mommy. Give me some money."

I got hopeful. Definitely time to make a move. I hunched my shoulders to look real small and pathetic. "I haven't eaten today. You got any change, even a nickel?"

Best to ask for crazy small change. Makes Reggies feel cheap if they don't give you something bigger.

"Joshua, stop pulling on Mommy's arm when I'm carrying heavy things."

Joshua kept tugging away and his mom was going to lose it, which was bad because that would mean she'd just bolt to her car.

"You don't have to," I said, making my voice crack a bit. "I'll be okay."

She put her bags down and began to dig around in her purse. Joshua wouldn't stop pulling on her coat, and then the other kid started asking for money.

"I don't have any change," I heard her mutter as the kids kept pulling away. "Stop it, you two. That's enough already, please!"

She pulled out two five-dollar bills. I swear. I couldn't believe it. She gave one to each kid, only the wind picked up and Joshua's brother dropped the bill and it blew away, with both kids tearing after it and their mom yelling at them to be careful and to stop. The bill went under a car and Joshua actually crawled under to get it.

"Joshua, get up. It's dirty and there's ice everywhere."

He obviously wasn't big on listening. He kept at it until he got the money, and ran over and gave the bills to me.

"You're legit, dude," I said to him. "Stay cool."

"Let's get going. Mommy's going to the car now. Daddy's at home waiting for us."

I guess they loved their dad since they ran to the car. Joshua turned and waved, and I waved back, and why not since he basically got me ten dollars. That did it for hawking today. I'd never been so loaded in my life — $15.50. This really was the best day ever.

I cut up to Union Street toward the hot dog vendor around the far side so I wouldn't have to deal with Creeper. I smelled the dogs before I even saw the cart. All the Undergrounders love these hot dogs, and if anybody has the coin to buy one they brag about it forever. I'd only eaten a few. One time a dad bought a hot dog for his little son and the kid threw it on the ground. The dad lost it and yelled and screamed and wouldn't let the little kid pick it up, and as the dad pulled his kid, who was having a total temper tantrum, I ran over and snatched it. I didn't get to choose my own toppings, though, so this would be way better.

"One hot dog," I ordered in a loud voice.

The man eyed me suspiciously. "Hot dogs ain't free," he said.

"No kidding," I shot back, holding out one of my five-dollar bills.

He squinted at me, making his face lopsided before cooking me up the dog.

"I see you here with the other boys. You ever go to school?" he asked me.

"Every day, sir. I'm in university."

"Another wise guy. All you kids are wise guys." He gave me my dog. "You want something to drink?"

The dog smelled so good I couldn't resist. "Give me a Coke," I said.

I loaded up on toppings until I could barely get my mouth around the hot dog. The heat from the hot dog warmed my mouth and my throat as I swallowed. It felt so good. If only this day could last forever. I ate as slowly as I could, wandering along the street past the railway station and around the back.

I tossed the hot dog wrapping and the pop can into the bushes and clambered down the steep hill past the old, rusting railway tracks. Only a loser brought food to the Underground, unless you were Rigger or Lewis or another big kid. I learned that the hard way when two kids jumped me for some bread and gave me two black eyes. Lewis called me raccoon-face until the dark circles went away.

Footprints in the snow dotted the way. A Reggie wouldn't notice the grey metal door in a million years. We called it the drawbridge, because drawbridges protect the only way in and out of a castle, and so did this. The Underground was our castle, and it protected us against the outside world, the weather, the cops, the Reggies, and most of all, Streeters.

I knocked the code as quietly as possible. Rigger would pound you if you made too much noise: two knocks — wait a second; two more — wait two seconds; three more knocks. The door opened a few centimetres.

"It's Mouse."

The door opened the rest of the way.

I was in.

Chapter 4

Brachy was guarding tonight. His name was a joke because it was short for Brachiosaurus, which was the biggest dinosaur ever, and Brachy was barely bigger than me and he was seventeen years old. I knew better than to talk to an older Undergrounder. I went to the elevator shaft and climbed down the rope ladder. The first rule of the Underground was pay Rigger, so I lined up behind a few others to pay the rent. Creeper was in front of me.

"Can you loan me tonight?" Creeper asked me.

Creeper was the biggest mooch in the Underground. I'd lent him three dollars over the past couple of months. Kiss that money goodbye, Lewis said to me when he heard, and he was right. Whenever I asked for it he always said he was broke.

"Can't do it," I said. "You saw me. I had to go to the parking lot."

I turned around to end the conversation. Soon it was my turn. Rigger was sitting in his armchair outside his store like he always was when it was rent time. I handed him a toonie, which was the change from the hot dog vendor.

Rigger reached into a bowl for my change. He rarely spoke to junior Undergrounders, and I just took my money and headed for my store. A few of the older kids were hanging out in the Executive Suites, which is what we called the row of stores leading from Rigger's. All the older kids took those. The Executive Suites were the biggest and also the warmest. Mine was way in the back. It was cold, and sometimes water got in. At least winter was dry.

We stayed together in one store to keep warm — Will, Rose, J.J. and me, that is. It's not that they were my friends, really, not like Lewis, and most of the time Will and Rose treated me pretty bad. Will and Rose were twins, although they didn't look alike. They were fourteen, but acted like they were five years older than me. J.J. was twelve like me, and he was a total whiner and practically the only Undergrounder I could pound, so he didn't give me a hard time. Of course, since me and Lewis were buds I didn't have much trouble with anyone.

"It's getting cold in here," I said, as I got into my sleeping bag. I didn't want Will to think I was afraid to talk.

"Thanks for the weather report," Will snapped. He was already in his sleeping bag.

I noticed a big bruise on his cheek. "What happened to—?" I never finished the question because Rose jumped in.

"Will got his butt kicked by some Streeter today," she said, as if it was funny.

"Shut up," he growled, pulling his sleeping bag under his chin. His right eye was also puffy and he had a cut on his chin.

"Who was it?" I asked.

"None of your business," Will said.

But I knew Rose would tell. "We were at the subway station hawking the rush-hour crowd when some Streeters told us to move. Will said we were there first, and this guy in an army jacket pounded Will something awful."

"Was he also wearing a green hat, with an American flag on the side?" I asked.

Rose nodded.

"That's W5. I wouldn't mess with him. He's a serious dude."

I delivered packages from Lewis to W5 about two or three times a week and I knew all about him.

"Hey, Mouse. Come on over for a sec."

That was Lewis calling for me. I hopped out of my sleeping bag double quick. I was dying to tell him about my day, anyway.

"It's cute the way the little doggy runs after his master," Rose said.

Sometimes she bugged me so much, and she had this way of talking slowly and real sarcastic about everything. Will was way bigger than me, so I couldn't do anything about him. Rose was tough too, and to be honest, although I'd never admit it, I was kind of scared of her.

So I just ignored her diss and raced over to Lewis's store, which was about five down from Rigger's. He was stretched out on his couch, as usual. He'd somehow been able to score a couch and lower it down. Only he and Rigger had something to sit on other than a milk box or cardboard. Sometimes Lewis let me sleep on his couch when he was out on business, which was a lot, especially lately.

He spotted me right off, as always.

"Yo, Mouse. What shakes in your world tonight?"

"Will got pounded by W5 at the subway."

His face darkened. "You were there?" he asked me.

"No. Rose told me about it. I didn't see nothin'."

Lewis laughed and patted the couch. "Sit down and relax. Was that a cold day, or what?"

There was nothing better than his couch. It was so soft. I told Lewis about my day, and every once in a while he'd whistle real low and his eyes would get wider. "You nicked that stuff all by yourself, for real?" he said, when I'd finished.

"Sure did. I admit I was a little scared at first."

He winked at me and put his arm around my shoulders. "I think you're ready for something more than just delivering packages. Give me a few days and I'll have something for you. You can help me out, and I can give you some money for it. Does that sound good?"

I nodded.

He stood up and held up his hands like a boxer, moving slowly to his left. This was my favourite game. I began to bob and weave, jabbing with my left like Lewis taught me, waiting for an opening. I knew I had no chance against Lewis, who was four years older and totally ripped, but it was fun to try.

I swung my right fist hard at his stomach, but he was too quick with his block and followed it up with a flurry of jabs. I covered up best I could until he wrapped me up in his arms and tossed me on the couch. That was his signal for game over. I scrambled to my feet ready to go back to my store. I learned the hard way about messing with Lewis. He was my best friend, but he had a wicked temper. Once I kept trying to box and he hit me for real on the side of the head. I got a huge lump and had a bad headache for a couple of days, but I deserved it for not listening.

"Don't get up," he said, pushing me onto the couch. "I gotta go out, and probably won't be back until morning. Got some business to deal with. Stay here and watch my stuff."

I couldn't believe my luck today. "Sure thing," I said, trying not to sound goofy. "I'll get my sleeping bag and be right back. Thanks, Lewis."

"No worries, Mouse. I may need you to take a package for me in the morning, so be ready. I'll catch you on the flip side of life."

Lewis grabbed his knapsack and left. I ran to get my bag.

"Where are you going?" Rose asked me.

"Lewis wants me to watch his stuff while he's out," I said.

"Out where?" she said.

"He's got business."

She had a laugh like a witch, real creepy, and she gave me an extra long one this time. She was so weird.

I wanted to diss her real bad. What was so funny about Lewis going out? I kept quiet, though, since Will was in such a bad mood, even for him. He could be real mean to his sister, but he'd protect her if anyone else tried. Besides, I had a couch to sleep on, while these losers were going to sleep on a cold floor.

My legs felt tired as I lay out on the couch, and my eyes got heavy real fast. Usually, I had trouble sleeping. I wasn't going to have much trouble tonight. The blisters on my feet bugged me a bit. Otherwise, it was like sleeping on a cloud or a bed of feathers.

I wouldn't ever forget this day — the best day of my life.

Chapter 5

Lewis must have had a lot of business because he wasn't back when Rigger rang the wakeup bell. I waited in line for the toilet. Rigger was strict about that: no doing your business except in the washroom. That rule I agreed with. Some guys were total pigs and they'd be peeing all over the place if they could. I never minded waiting. It was worth it to have a real toilet at least once a day.

"Hurry up," Fitzy said, banging on the door.

"Don't rush me. It's a masterpiece," Happy D replied.

He was a bizarre guy, always talking about gross stuff like poo and vomit, like a four-year-old. Lewis thought Fitzy hung with Happy D because he was a good fighter.

"We need to do our own masterpieces!" Fitzy yelled back.

I knew he was only pretending to be mad.

"I'm telling Rigger you're hogging the can," Creeper said. "If I end up having to stay past nine and pay extra I'm gonna go ballistic."

"I'd like to see you try," Happy D called out in a cheerful voice.

"You're such a puke," Creeper said.

Puke was our favourite dissing word.

J.J. joined the line behind me. "Where're you going today?" I asked. We usually went hawking together, and I wanted to know the plan for this afternoon, after I went skating at the rink.

"I'm gonna try the Theatre," he replied glumly.

"I wasted a day there not too long ago," I offered.

"So what."

That wasn't too friendly. I changed the subject. "You hear about Will?"

J.J. scrunched his eyes and crinkled his nose. "I heard he got in a fight or something," he said, as if he wasn't interested.

I knew he was. Will was his hero. "He got pounded by W5. You know him? Wears an army jacket. Will got a big black eye and is in serious pain. Didn't he tell you?" I figured it would bug J.J. to know I knew something about Will that he didn't.

J.J. stared at me. "He wasn't the only one."

"W5 pounded you too?"

"No, spaz. These puke streeters stole my money when I was coming here last night, which is why I was late. I took two of them out, only there were five and they got me down on the ground."

He didn't look too beat up to me. J.J. exaggerated — a lot. He'd freak if you called him on it, and besides, I didn't care. "Are you okay?" I assumed that was the right thing to ask.

"I toughed it out. I'm gonna get mine back. You

wait and see. Those pukes are toast."

The door opened, and Creeper went in. I bet J.J. just threw the money on the ground and wet his pants. He'd never fight.

Creeper took a long time, and I figured out why when it was my turn. He always stunk the place up. I did my business as fast as I could and got out.

Normally, I'd go out with J.J., or Rose and Will, or one of the other junior Undergrounders, and we'd hit the streets together. It felt awesome to be on my own today. I had twelve dollars in my pocket, and I could play hockey all day if I wanted. I even knew a place where I could sharpen my skates. It would cost four bucks, but I had the money; and besides, I had to.

I went to Lewis's store first. He'd said last night he needed me to help him with a package, so I sat back on the couch and waited. I must have drifted off to sleep for a minute because I woke up and heard voices from outside the store.

"Don't be such a turd. I've been planning this for a week."

That sounded like Fitzy.

"I don't feel like it."

That was definitely Happy D.

"I'm gonna hang by the television station," Happy D said.

"You're going to throw away a chance to make two hundred bucks this morning!" Fitzy hissed.

Happy D yawned and looked at Fitzy with a big grin. Fitzy stepped forward. "I need your help, dude. I can't do this myself. We planned it out. It's now or never. Come on."

"Do it yourself."

"Let's get going, you lazy puke."

That's when Fitzy turned and saw me, and his face went all white as if all the blood was drained out, and his eyes were wide open. I didn't bother waiting. I tried to bolt out down the hall to the ladder, only Fitzy was too fast and caught me.

"A little mouse is stickin' his noise into my business," Fitzy raged.

My heart was beating so bad I swear I could hear it.

"You say a word to anyone and I'll smash that mouse head of yours, I swear," Fitzy said into my ear.

"I didn't hear nothin'," I stammered. "I just heard voices and Happy D said he was tired."

"You're lying," Fitzy said, "and I'm gonna pound you until the truth comes out."

"Why so hostile, Fitzy, my friend and bosom pal?"

Fitzy let my collar go and stepped away. Lewis laughed at me and flopped down on the couch. I backed up into the store to get closer to Lewis. No way Fitzy would take Lewis on.

"This snooping little puke was listening to me and Happy D having a private conversation," Fitzy accused.

Before Lewis could ask me I said, "I didn't hear a word. I was waiting for you on the couch, like you told me to. Fitzy said he wanted Happy D to come with him, and Happy D didn't wanna. That's it. I swear."

Fitzy glared at me, but I could tell he wouldn't dare do anything with Lewis there.

"You promise not to say anything about this — and I mean to anyone — not even Rigger?" Lewis said to me.

I nodded like a million times.

Lewis laughed, then pulled a package out of his knapsack and handed it to me. "I need you to take this to the subway station. Scrunchy Face will be there soon, so you'd better get going."

We called W5's friend Scrunchy Face because that's what his face looked like — all scrunched together. I didn't like him. He was always mean to me, and usually roughed me up for no reason.

"No problem, Lewis. I'll go right now."

He slapped me on the shoulder. I didn't even look at Fitzy or Happy D. The subway station was a bit out of the way from the rink, but not too bad. Rigger was on his chair as usual, his legs hanging over the armrest.

Rigger glanced at his watch. "Cutting it close, Mouse. Ten minutes to clear out."

Creeper ran past, followed by J.J., Will and Rose. Will's eye was swollen almost shut, and there was a big black smudge under it.

"You coming?" J.J. yelled to me.

"You go ahead, and I'll meet up with you."

As I started up the ladder, I looked down the hall and saw Fitzy and Lewis talking together. Fitzy was obviously up to something. Why would Lewis be interested? He was way too legit to hang with Fitzy.

The cold air hit my nose and I felt my snot begin to run. The cold always did that to me. It was so irritating and everyone bugged me about it. It wasn't my fault I didn't have a tissue. I climbed up the hill to the street and headed toward the subway to drop off the package. On the way I could cut over to Franklin and get some Chinese buns for breakfast. I was starving, as usual.

After my errands were done, I made myself forget all about Fitzy, Rigger, and the whole Underground. I had skates and was going to spend the morning at the rink. The gloves I stole fit perfectly and the hockey sweater made me warmer too. My feet were cold, but I could take it. Snow began to fall lightly. It was actually kind of pretty with the snowflakes drifting in slow motion to the ground.

This was going to be another great day. How couldn't it be? A great sleep, money in my pocket — and hockey!

Chapter 6

I loved the rasping sound of my blades digging into the ice. I could have done without the cold wind blowing in my face or the pain in my feet from the blisters that had broken even with the Band-Aids. But I ignored all that as I headed up ice, imagining it was game seven, overtime, Stanley Cup Final, with the puck deep in our end.

I imagined a forechecker coming hard and I swerved at the hash marks into the slot to avoid him, cutting up the middle into the neutral zone. Time to end this, I said to myself. At centre I did a little shoulder fake to throw off the D, dangled the puck, and then about five feet from the blue line slowed a bit, bobbed my head left and right, and then flicked the puck forward and leapt high in the air. The clueless defencemen were left behind by my move. For fun I dropped my stick low and flipped the puck onto the blade, spun around and shoved it under the crossbar.

Arms held high, I closed my eyes as I curved outside toward centre. What would the Undergrounders say about me scoring the overtime goal to win the Cup?

That would shut Fitzy up. Another gust of wind reminded me how cold it was, though. I must have been out there for two hours. I'd promised J.J. that I'd meet him at the Theatre, and it wouldn't hurt to get some hawking in. I could ditch my stuff in my hiding spot too. I grabbed the puck and headed in.

I'd barely got my skates off when that scraggly janitor walked up the hall, pushing a bucket by the mop handle. He stopped in the middle of the room and stared at me so long I started to think I'd done something wrong.

"I didn't play too long . . . did I?"

He shook his head and began to mop the floor. "You skate good," he said.

A bit random, but I said thanks all the same. Then he reached into his pocket and dropped a toonie into my lap.

"Why are you . . . giving me this?"

His head jerked sideways at me. "I know what it means for boy to skate alone in morning. No school — no home. I see you around. I like to help."

Before I could say anything he spun around and pushed the bucket back down the hall. I couldn't believe my luck. I was on a total roll, as Lewis would say.

I went to the Theatre to hide my skates and stuff, and headed around to the front.

I spotted J.J.'s red coat straight away. He was at the front entrance. Will and Rose were farther down the street. I walked toward them real slow, and then jerked my head up as if I was surprised to see them.

"Yo, J.J. What's up?"

He made a sour face. "Nothin'. Too cold. Nobody's even looking at me. I've made fifty cents all morning."

I nodded at Will and Rose down at the far doors.

"They got zip too," J.J. said. "Brutal day. I could eat my left arm — my right one too."

I don't know what possessed me. I must have lost my mind or something. "Let's go to Winston's and get some Chinese buns." I held up the toonie the janitor had given me.

J.J.'s grin was too big for his face. "You da man, Mouse. You da man."

Then I got a surprise. "You doing good today, eh, Mouse?" Will said in a real friendly way. He and Rose had joined us.

Decision time. Will barely tolerated me, and Rose wasn't much better.

"Give it a rest, Will," Rose said. "It's his money."

Her arms were wrapped around her chest, her thin bluish lips pressed tightly together. Will was puffing on a cigarette butt.

I surprised myself a second time. "We can all go. I found this on the sidewalk. Total lucky day. Let's go eat."

I turned and headed toward Winston's and didn't bother looking to see if they were behind me. If food was involved, they'd come. I knew it was the money, but all the same it felt good to have them following me for a change. Anyway, all the Undergrounders worshipped Winston's buns. They had different types. My favourite was coconut with lemon filling, and they cost fifty cents each. We went there because Winston usually let us in. Lots of places didn't.

Winston was at the counter, a short Chinese man with stubbly black hair. I'd never seen him smile.

"Can we have four coconut buns, please," I said loudly, happy that they'd let me do the ordering. They could eat what I liked.

He put four in a bag. "No eating inside," he said. "Out."

"But we paid for them," Will said.

Winston held the bag to his chest.

"We'll eat them outside," I said. "The fresh air is nice."

It was hard to tell, but I could swear Winston actually smiled. We Undergrounders had a bet that whoever made Winston laugh would get a dollar from everyone. I guess I was making progress! He put the bag on the counter and turned away. I snatched it double quick and hightailed it out of there, then we all huddled together to eat. They were still warm — totally awesome. For a second it wasn't that cold — but only for a second.

"Let's go see if the vent is free," Will said when we were done.

I followed this time. It was nice to be included in the group. Since my mom died I spent most of my time alone, even when I was in the Underground. The others barely talked to me, except Lewis, of course. The vents weren't too far away, about five minutes. We all turned the corner together.

The vents were prime spots when it was cold. Hot air from the subway pumped up through the steel grates, and you could lie on them in the coldest night of the year and still be warm. I'd only been on them twice. Three men and a woman were lying across them. None were moving so I figured they were sleeping.

"Nice plan," Rose said.

"Shut up," Will snapped. "Not my fault. Dumb drunks."

"Maybe we should go back to the Underground," J.J. said.

"It's not five o'clock yet, stupid," Will said.

"Yeah. Well, so what?" J.J. muttered.

Will slapped his thigh real hard. "I'm spaced. Must be this cold. Let's do the mall."

Rose looked unhappy. "We got kicked out last time, and I don't feel like having everyone staring at me like I'm a piece of garbage. The security guards will be on us the minute we walk through the door."

"We won't have to deal with security. It'll be fine."

I'd never seen Rose so sad. I thought she might actually cry. "I'm really cold, Will. What should we do?" She sounded desperate.

"Trust me, Rose," Will said gently. "Let's go to the mall. I have a spot where they won't find us. I got it all figured out. Me and Creeper found it." He flicked his head at me and J.J. "You guys in?"

I certainly didn't have anywhere else to go. J.J. and I nodded. The mall was a good fifteen-minute walk. It was the only big one downtown. The security guards didn't like street kids too much, and most of the time you got chased out real quick, and I didn't go often because of that. But even though I didn't think much of Will's plan, I liked marching across town in a group — our own crew. It made me feel safer.

Chapter 7

We walked right past the mall entrance. I didn't dare question Will, though — didn't want to push my luck.

Rose wasn't so shy. "We gonna get into the mall by climbing the walls like Spiderman?"

Will didn't answer, but kept going until we got to a blue metal door. "I'll open this a crack and you jump in one at a time. Wait for me in there. Don't go up the stairs." Before we had a chance to say anything, he stuck a thin piece of metal into the side of the door and pried it open. I'd passed that door a million times and never thought that it could be opened from the outside. I had to hand it to Will and Creeper for figuring this out.

Rose went first, me second, and then J.J. came next and smashed right into us.

"Smooth move, doofus," Rose barked.

"Where are we?" he gasped.

"Maybe a stairwell," Rose replied.

"No kidding, doofus."

"Then why'd you ask?"

"Why are you so dumb?"

Will came in. "Shut up," he hissed. "You guys are so lame. I'm gonna check things out. Stay down here and be quiet and try not to be unbelievably stupid like you usually are."

We waited for at least two minutes. Naturally, Rose and J.J. started in on each other, and finally I couldn't take it and went up the stairs a bit just to get away. One flight up I found a door with a handle. I pushed on it and stuck my head out. I could hear the buzz of the mall crowd.

"Mouse," a voice hissed.

I shut the door. Will grabbed me by the shoulders and pulled me back against the wall. "I told you to wait for me. Do you understand English?"

I guess he'd already forgotten who'd paid for his Chinese bun. It didn't seem like a good time to remind him. "Rose and J.J. were losing it and I was coming to get you."

Will let me go. I knew he'd buy that. "Tell those losers to come up here," he ordered.

I didn't have to because they must have heard us and were climbing up.

"What are we doing here?" Rose said to Will.

Will smiled, which he did when he was bragging about something. "Creeper and I found this stairway. We jammed the door so we could get in from the outside. It's brilliant. Now follow me real quiet. This leads to an office tower that's attached to the mall. It's warmer up there."

He led us to the fifth floor and slumped to the floor. I didn't need to be asked. It felt great to get off my feet. The blisters were burning me big time. J.J. fell asleep in like two seconds; Rose was next; so there was me and Will being the only ones awake. I had to give him props for finding this place, but I wasn't going to start talking to him like he was some great guy. I took off my coat and scrunched it into a pillow and lay down. Unfortunately, the blisters on my feet were really stinging and keeping me up. I took off my shoes and socks and pulled out a couple of Band-Aids from my pocket.

"Do I really have to look at your stupid feet?" Will said. "I don't wanna throw up my bun."

"My shoes are killing me," I said, pointing to my blisters.

He peered closer. "How'd your shoes do that?"

I shrugged, got to work on my Band-Aids, and then lay down myself. Undergrounders don't get many chances to sleep in a warm place during the day, and I didn't want to waste a second.

○ ○ ○

A lady's scream woke me up and sent my heart beating like a maniac. I jumped to my feet. Standing by the door, obviously terrified, was a woman, hands balled at her chest. She had a big plastic label with her picture on it hanging on a chain around her neck.

We all stared at each other for a few seconds. In a real shaky voice she said, "This is not a bedroom. You all have to leave right away."

I guess the others were as scared and groggy as me

since no one moved or said a word. The lady moved slowly to the door.

"I will call security if you don't leave the premises immediately. You scared me half to death. Go home."

Why would she be scared? Will was the first one down the stairs, with Rose and J.J. close behind. That's when I remembered my shoes were still off. I picked them up and our eyes met. She didn't look so scared now. More like sad.

"People use these stairs sometimes when the elevator is slow. It's not a good idea to be here. You can get in a lot of trouble."

For some reason there was a ton of saliva in my throat and I had to swallow a couple of times. She pointed at my feet. "Put your shoes on. Not a good day to walk around barefoot."

I sat on a stair and stuffed my feet into my shoes as quickly as I could. She sounded kind of nice, and I began to feel bad about freaking her out. "We didn't mean to scare you," I said. "We just needed to get out of the cold. The door was open. I'm . . . sorry."

She folded her arms and nodded. "You should hurry to catch your friends," she said softly.

As I walked past I could see the picture on her card more clearly. She looked a bit younger, all smiling and pretty. Her name was Jenna. It sucked that we couldn't come back. What a perfect warm spot, even better than the vents. The tile floor wasn't even that cold. Will would be plenty mad about it; Creeper too.

When I came out I got another surprise, although I

should have expected it. They'd all ditched me. I looked around a bit and didn't see anyone. It hurt to think they wouldn't wait for me. As long as I had money they'd wait! I wished I had that toonie back. Then I would have eaten all four buns. One bun didn't put much of a dent into the pain in my stomach. The problem with hockey is it makes you hungry.

Even worse, it was starting to get dark, which meant there wasn't much time to hawk, and it was dangerous to be out after dark. Lewis had warned me about that a million times.

Of course I still had eight dollars. After what happened, I decided I could treat myself. Which meant it was hot dog time! Will, Rose and J.J. were going to love to hear that I had a dog, and you can bet I was going to tell them this time. Teach them to ditch me. I hurried along in case the vendor had left.

"You're becoming a regular customer," he said.

"I'll have the usual," I said, as if I had one every day.

When the dog was ready he wrapped it in a paper napkin and handed it to me. This time I loaded it up with pickles and hot peppers, and the burn in my throat warmed me up so nice, I almost ordered another one.

"I'll see you tomorrow," I said to the vendor.

He nodded slowly and turned away, and I headed off to the Underground.

Chapter 8

I wound up at the blue line and let it fly. The puck nicked the crossbar and bounced in. I'd been here every day for sixteen straight days — didn't miss even one — skating, shooting, stickhandling, for hours and hours. And I was getting pretty good, even though it was a little boring. You can only play so many imaginary games. Maybe I was extra lonely because Lewis still hadn't come back; neither had Fitzy. Rumours were flying around the Underground. J.J. was saying they'd both been shot. I knew he was an idiot, but I was getting worried.

I gathered the puck out of the net and carried it down to the far end and was about to let another shot rip when I heard some voices.

"There's no one here. Let's do this, boys."

I curved real slow around the boards and snuck a look. This was ugly — a bunch of Reggies coming to play. How'd they get off school? All my stuff was in the change room where they'd be putting on their skates. I figured it was best to wait until they all came out and then slip away.

I took a few more shots, although I wasn't into it anymore. One shot went over the net and bounced off the fencing into the corner. As I retrieved the puck, three kids came on. It was the same bunch that played the day I stole my skates. I saw the friendly kid, Rasheed, and the angry one, Derrick, and the big one, Collin, too.

"Hit me, Rasheed. I'm feelin' it," Collin yelled at the blue line, and Rasheed slid the puck over. Collin one-timed it and missed the net by ten feet — and he let out a huge laugh. "I had high hopes for that shot," he said.

"I'm surprised you actually hit the puck," Rasheed joked.

"Me too," Collin replied.

It was kind of funny, especially the way Collin said it. He raced to get the puck and then flung it blindly toward Rasheed. It went way wide and slid all the way down the ice. Not exactly what I wanted because now I had to pass it back or look like a doofus. Rasheed held his stick up, and I rifled it to him.

He took the pass easily, which showed some skill. Circling at centre, he flipped it high at the net before cruising toward me.

"You want to play with us?"

What a spot to be in. Hanging with Reggies? But how lame would I look if I just left? And would it really be so terrible if I played for a few minutes? "I guess. If you need a guy. I have to go soon, but . . ." I shrugged as if I didn't care.

"Sounds good." He turned and cupped his hands.

"Let's play two-on-two until everyone comes out. You two against us."

Derrick circled the net and passed to Collin.

"I'll take Collin," Rasheed said to me. "You cover Derrick, and watch out 'cause he's fast."

Collin passed to Derrick at the red line. I guessed Derrick would try to outskate me, and sure enough he charged wide to the left and up boards. Since Rasheed had told me to watch his speed I was ready, and all I had to do was cut him off and strip the puck away.

It slid down toward the corner. The ice was real choppy down there, and it was tough to dig it out in one motion but I pulled it off. Derrick chopped at the puck as I went around the net. I had to lose this guy. I put on the brakes and spun back behind the net in one motion and Derrick sailed past me. I darted up the other side. A quick look told me Derrick wasn't hustling back, so it was a two-on-one.

Collin waited at centre. "You got no chance. Can't get by me. I'm the wall."

From what I could tell the wall was doing a pretty good standing-still impression. I turned on the jets and by the blue line was in alone. Rasheed banged his stick on the ice, I backhanded a pass to him, and he blasted it off the post.

Rasheed pretended he'd scored a great goal and threw his stick over his head, and I skated backward to our end.

"Sick move," Rasheed said to me. "Where do you play?"

I didn't understand. "I play here."

He laughed. He always seemed to be laughing. "No, I mean what team do you play for?"

He meant what league team, and he obviously thought I was a Reggie too. I wondered what he'd say if he knew who I really was. Anyway, I didn't know the names of any teams, so I couldn't make something up. "I don't play for a team. I just fool around."

Collin and Derrick were attacking, and we had to stop talking. Derrick had the puck wide left. Collin faked up the middle and swerved to the right. I covered him, and Rasheed slid over to pressure Derrick. He kept going to the outside and crossed the blue line. Collin cut back over and called for it. Derrick tried a back pass and this time I was able to step in and take the puck.

Collin and Derrick had me cornered against the boards.

"Hey, over here."

Rasheed was wide open in the slot in front of our net waving his stick over his head. I slid the puck between Collin's feet, right to him. Rasheed made as if he was going to take it himself up the left side, but Derrick cut him off and Rasheed turned back. Collin drifted forward, keeping an eye on me.

Rasheed passed it back to me and slowly crept up the right side. All of a sudden he cut in between Derrick and Collin. I led him perfect with a pass and quick as a flash he was in on a breakaway. I applauded him by slapping the ice with my stick.

"Love that pass," Rasheed said to me, as Collin

went to retrieve the puck from the net. "Who'd you play for last year?"

"Like I said, I don't really play for a team. I did when I was younger."

"Are you peewee this year?" he asked suddenly.

I knew peewee was an age group, but I couldn't remember exactly how old you had to be. He eyed me closer. Lucky for me, I didn't have to answer because a pile of his friends roared onto the ice and distracted him. There looked to be eight or nine guys. It was time for me to go.

"I . . . um . . . should get going," I said to Rasheed. "You guys don't need me. Bye."

I didn't wait for him to say another word. I just skated real quick to the door and left.

"See ya!" Rasheed yelled out.

In no time I'd ripped off my skates and tossed them in the bag. That's when I remembered my puck. I was so nervous I'd left without it. I'd lost my puck for no reason. *Loser!* No way I was going to put my skates back on. I was so mad at myself I didn't notice Rasheed at the door.

"Hey, you forgot your puck. Here you go."

He tossed it to me. "You visiting your uncle again?"

"Um . . . yeah . . . my uncle."

"Next time you visit, come on out. Maybe we'll be here."

"Okay. Maybe."

I waved goodbye as he left.

Nice guy. Anyway, it was time to get going. I was

really hungry after all that hockey. The stomach was rumbling something fierce. For a lark I looked in the garbage can, and my eyes nearly jumped out of my head. Some loser had thrown out half a sandwich, and I mean a big one. Almost laughing at my luck, I reached down to get it.

"Did you lose something?"

I spun around, holding the sandwich behind my back.

Rasheed grinned.

"I dropped a loonie into the garbage," I said. "Lame move. Can't be bothered looking — too gross in there."

Rasheed kept on grinning. That guy was permanently happy. "I forgot to tell you. This was a P.A. day, and we're usually not here. But we have a regular Saturday morning pickup game around ten o'clock. Feel free to come out. Me and you make a good team — and we can burn Collin and Derrick again."

He had a way of saying things like that without insulting someone. Of course, there was no way. "Not sure if I can. Like I said, I don't live around here. Maybe. I'll try."

"Awesome." He flashed his grin. "See ya — again."

I let out a deep breath. How embarrassing would that have been, to get caught eating out of the garbage. Then I could never have come back. Undergrounders understood that sometimes you had to raid the can; a Reggie would think I was a freak.

I looked at the sandwich. It was half eaten. I felt sick

looking at it, even dizzy. Before my mom died I wouldn't have touched someone else's food, let alone eat it. But my stomach won out. It always did. I ran out of there so Rasheed and his friends wouldn't see me, and after one bite I couldn't stop.

It tasted so good.

Chapter 9

Rose woke me up with her coughing. She'd coughed like a maniac all night with Will telling her to shut up every five minutes. He kept me up more than her. He's such a pain — not her fault she has a cough. Even though she made fun of me, she wasn't mean, at least not like him.

I heard voices from the Executive Suites, and they got louder and louder. One voice rose above the others — Fitzy! Could that mean Lewis was back? I scrambled out of my sleeping bag, put on my coat, and ran into the hall.

"What's Mouse all excited about?" Creeper said as I ran past.

I ignored him and went to Lewis's store. There he was, lying on his couch, his feet hanging over the end, an arm across his eyes.

"Lewis, where've you been? You've been gone like forever!"

He didn't answer. I walked in slowly and peered over his head. He took his arm away.

"Get lost, Mouse. I'm not in the mood."

"But I just wanted to ask . . ."

"I said beat it," he snarled.

Lewis never talked to me like that. What happened to him? I left, which turned out to be a good idea as Fitzy was telling the others what Lewis wouldn't tell me.

"It was gonna be so easy — the perfect plan." Even Rigger was crowding around. "This bud of mine works at a computer store. On Mondays he closes the place. We arranged that the alarm would be off and the back door unlocked. Me and Lewis got in around midnight and before you know it we had like dozens of iPods and phones and even some cash. It was wicked."

He laughed and licked his lips. "Of course, that jerk forgot to turn off the alarm because all of a sudden it went off like a friggin' siren. I tell ya, I almost had a heart attack."

I just couldn't help myself. "What did Lewis do?" I blurted.

Fitzy and a few others looked over at me like I was a Martian before he continued. "We took off and ran right into five cops charging in through the back door, and then another five or so came in from the front. We had a freakin' army of cops on us, and the next thing I know, me and Lewis are handcuffed and thrown into the back of a cop car."

"Did they give you a phone call?" Happy D said.

"Yeah. I called the President of the United States."

"What did he say?"

"I didn't actually call him, you moron . . ."

"Get on with it," Brachy said.

"Anyone got some food?" Fitzy asked. "I'm freakin' starving. We haven't eaten in like two days."

Brachy handed him some bread. Fitzy gnawed on it like an animal, and kept telling the story.

"We spent a night in jail — no kidding — I mean for real. One drunk dude punched Lewis in the head for no reason. It was crazed. I thought we were dead, I swear. Then we go to a courtroom before a real judge. He had a black robe and stuff just like you see on TV Because me and Lewis are under eighteen we got a real lawyer — no kidding — our very own lawyer. She wore a black gown too.

"I worked out a story for Lewis the night before. I got him to practise until he got it real good. It was my idea to say we were brothers living on the street and that our dad used to beat us and we were starving and only wanted food."

Lewis brushed past me. "Did you tell them how you cried when our lawyer said we could be charged as adults and go to adult jail for ten years?"

Fitzy snorted. "You're dreaming. I saved your butt and you know it."

"You saved my butt!" Lewis was steaming mad. "Your crazy plan got me arrested."

They looked real hateful at each other, and I thought Lewis would pound him out. I knew he wanted to, which is why I still couldn't get why Lewis went with Fitzy to that store in the first place. Lewis knew Fitzy was a total goofball.

Lewis waved the back of his hand at Fitzy and left for the ladder without saying a word, which I thought was totally sick. I had to remember that move the next time J.J. or Will was bugging me.

"The guy kinda lost it," Fitzy said quietly. "Speaking of crying, he was practically sobbing in jail when the guy went after him. I pushed him away, and look at the thanks I get. What a jerk."

He laughed and finished off the bread. I knew he was lying about Lewis. No way he'd cry.

"The best part is our lawyer buys my story and convinces the judge that jail is too rough and is a bad environment. The judge agrees to send us to a halfway house."

I knew about those. They're houses for young kids who get into trouble with the law. Lewis says they're run by do-gooder social workers who think they can solve everyone's problems by talking and bogus stuff like that.

"You should've seen me. 'Oh, thank you, judge,' I said. 'I just need a chance to turn my life around.' Anyway, as soon as we could, me and Lewis climb out a window at night and we were gone. Stupid place was miles from here. It took a day to walk back."

Rigger stepped forward. "You didn't tell the cops about the Underground, did you?"

Rigger could get scary mean when he wanted to. Fitzy got all laughing and slapped his thigh as if that was the funniest thing he'd ever heard.

"No chance. I never said nothing. I played it real

smooth. 'I live on the streets, Your Honour,' I said, which is what you call them judges — Your Honour. More like Your Idiot if you ask me."

"And Lewis?" Rigger asked in a low voice. "Did you hear him say anything?"

Fitzy shrugged. "Don't know. He got kinda weird on me. I didn't hear him say anything, but how can I be sure?"

Rigger growled and his left eye got squinty. I couldn't take Fitzy's lying.

"Lewis wouldn't do that," I said. I was too crazy mad to stop myself. "No way he told the cops about us. That's a joke. Why would he? He came back here, didn't he?"

"The little bitty mouse is all angry-wangry," Fitzy mocked in a baby voice. "Are you all sad 'cause your hero turns out to be a crybaby?"

I wanted to smash his ugly stupid face to pieces. But he was sixteen years old and way bigger. He'd pound me before I could even hit him once. I copied Lewis and turned my back and left. I slammed my foot into each rung as I climbed up to the street level.

Lewis was sitting on the stool beside the door smoking a cigarette. He could blow the sickest smoke rings, and even make one ring go through another. He wouldn't teach me because he said smoking's bad for you. But he smoked. Sometimes I didn't understand him.

I peered out the door to make sure the coast was clear. "I'll see ya later," I said, as nice as I could.

"Take care of yourself, Mouse," he said. He didn't sound that angry now.

I swallowed hard. "Did that guy hurt you . . . I mean in jail . . . the drunk guy who hit you?"

He smiled a bit. "Fitzy can exaggerate stuff, especially with a crowd around him. I can handle myself."

"No one would mess with you, Lewis," I said. Which was true. I bet even Rigger was afraid of him.

"So where are you off to this lovely morning?"

That sounded like the old Lewis. "I'm gonna go to the rink. I've been there every day for more than two weeks. I even played with some Reggies yesterday."

I knew I should not have told him that.

"Don't get mixed up with regular kids. You can't trust them. They're not like us."

"I know. It was only for five minutes."

He looked at me for a second, and then laughed. "Five minutes won't kill you."

I laughed too. We were buds again. I'd missed him so much. I think I'd actually pretended he wasn't really gone.

"You hungry?" he asked.

"Maybe a little."

He got up. "Follow me. I have a can of tuna and some bread. Besides, I need to talk to you about some business I need taken care of."

I followed him back down into the Underground.

Chapter 10

I stopped counting the number of times I flip-flopped between going to the Market and playing hockey with Rasheed and his friends. First I convinced myself that I was too tired; then I was going to hunt for beer and liquor bottles to return for the deposit money; next I decided Rasheed didn't really want me to play because he didn't know me. I must have come up with a million reasons not to play — and here I was in front of the rink, more nervous than I'd ever been in my life. I was so scared of these guys. And why? Reggies weren't tough like Undergrounders. They'd barely last a day on the streets before running home to Mommy.

Rasheed must have spotted me through the window because he opened the door and waved. That left me no choice and I headed in.

"Awesome!" Rasheed beamed. "We only have seven guys. Now we can play four-on-four."

I smiled back, although I think my face came out looking kind of goofy.

He tugged on my shoulder. "Throw your stick to

the outside when we're picking sides and I'll make sure we're on the same team," he whispered.

"Okay," I mumbled, not sure what he meant.

"Hey, guys. We've got even teams now," Rasheed declared.

His friends barely looked over. They didn't seem too stoked to see me. Collin kept looking at me, though, which made me even more nervous and self-conscious; and then he asked the one question I dreaded.

"So what team do you play for?"

Everyone heard that and was waiting for me to answer. "I was telling Rasheed . . . I just fool around here, at the rink . . ."

Collin fired a few more questions, and I felt my face flush from all the attention. "Are you peewee or minor peewee? Do you play AAA? Where do you live?"

Rasheed, Derrick and the others laughed.

"Why don't you ask him another ten questions at once," Rasheed said.

Collin joined in the laughter and pointed at me. "I need some info on the kid that smoked me so bad that I looked like I belonged in house league," he said.

I had a million things to do, and here I was trying to play hockey with a bunch of Reggies who would freak if they found out who I really was.

"You missed one question," Rasheed said. "What's your name?"

"Jonathon."

"And . . . you don't play for any team . . . that's what you told Rasheed?" Derrick said.

These questions were bad news. I thought of running, until an idea came into my brain from out of nowhere. "We moved from Brentwood. I used to play for the Hawks. I couldn't find a team, so . . . I decided to practise here when I visit my uncle and wait until next year."

"You couldn't find a team because you missed the tryouts in April?" Collin asked.

I nodded, and thank God that satisfied him.

Rasheed stood up. "Hurry up, slugs. I need to dangle a few of you. It's good for my morale given we've lost every game so far this season."

"We've got no business playing AA," Collin said, and laughed in a way that I guessed meant he didn't really care.

"We could win — if all the guys wanted to," Derrick growled.

"We can't score — that's the problem. All we need is someone to put the puck in the net," Rasheed said. That was the first time I heard Rasheed say something serious.

"I keep telling you to move me up to forward and I'll fill the net," Collin said, thumping his chest.

His friends all started dissing Collin real good about that, but it was different from what I was used to because it was kind of nice at the same time, like in a way that made it obvious everyone liked him. I hadn't heard boys speak to each other like that in a long time; we didn't in the Underground. I guess I'd sort of forgotten how Reggies talk.

We all piled onto the ice and began skating around and shooting at the nets. Pretty soon Collin shouted, "Sticks at centre!" I stopped next to him, as the other guys kept goofing around.

"Don't be fooled," Collin said. "They usually really listen to me."

I was still so nervous I couldn't think of what to say.

"That was kind of a joke," Collin said.

My brain finally unlocked itself. "I was gonna wait for something a little better," I said.

He laughed. "I'm not warmed up yet," he said, tossing his stick on the ice, "and how can I when it's like twenty below?"

A few of the guys came up and tossed their sticks on top of Collin's. Rasheed caught my eye and pointed to his stick and I dropped mine on top of his.

"I'll divvy them up," Rasheed said, and he began dividing the sticks into two piles. He threw his together with mine. That's when I understood. This is how they picked teams. It was supposed to be random. I retrieved my stick and followed Rasheed to the far end.

"This here is Jacob," Rasheed said, pointing to a tall kid with a Pittsburgh Penguins tuque. "We play on the same line with Derrick."

Jacob tilted his head toward me. The other kid held out his glove and I tapped it with mine. "I'm Matthew. Rasheed tells me you can really bring it."

I felt myself blush. I hated that. So lame!

"Do you play with Rasheed too?" It's all I could think of saying.

"Play with these guys?" Matthew said, as if that was ridiculous.

Rasheed laughed. "We didn't want him, so he had to play with the Red Wings — who just happen to be the best team in the league."

"Nothing can stop the C-Train," Collin roared, as he powered down the right side.

"After him, boys," Rasheed declared.

Matthew stepped up to play forward and so did Jacob. I drifted back to play D. Rasheed rode Collin into the boards and the puck squirted free. It squibbed into the corner and I was able to scoop it up and drift behind the net. Matthew was camped out at the wall by the hash marks, and I snapped a pass over. Matthew took a few steps, looked quickly to his left and then backhanded it back to me.

Derrick swung over to forecheck. Instinctively, I did a head fake, slipped the puck between his skates, and pushed hard to the outside. That Matthew could play; he anticipated my move and was already cutting across their blue line. I passed to him again and he motored over the line down the left side and then dropped it for Rasheed. The slot was wide open, and I scooted in unnoticed by the defenceman who was focused on Jacob. Rasheed feathered a sweet pass right onto my stick.

The defencemen left Jacob and tried to poke-check me. I shifted the puck to my backhand and took it wide right. Out of the corner of my eye I spotted Matthew, who must have continued on to the net. I slid it over and he banged it off the post.

"He scores!" Rasheed yelled, and he lifted his stick over his head.

I would have shot the puck into the net. Lucky Matthew shot first. I had forgotten that you had to hit the post to score.

Matthew came up from behind and thumped me on the back. "The kid can bring it," he said, in a big dramatic voice.

"Nice goal," I said — and I guess it was.

"You gotta at least try to slow us down," Rasheed said to the other team.

"Teams are way too stacked," Collin complained.

"Let's play to five and we'll switch it up," Rasheed said.

It didn't take us more than five minutes to do that. Playing with Matthew and Rasheed was magic. They were always where I wanted them to be, and I would get the pass, right on my stick, at the exact right moment. Jacob kind of got in the way, but we basically ignored him. On the last goal, Rasheed, me, and Matthew must have passed it ten times around the net before I snuck behind a player at the far post and drilled it off the post before he could turn around.

The guy obviously didn't like that much and he swung his stick at the puck and banged me right on the shin just after I scored. The pain took my breath away. No way I was crying, though. Undergrounders don't cry when they get hurt. I turned away and wiped my eyes, pretending I had some dirt in them, and ignored the pain.

No one saw me — or at least nobody said anything.

"Sick moves, Jonathon," Rasheed said.

We punched gloves.

"The J-Man is on fire," Matthew said a few times.

I had to laugh. These guys were kind of funny. That was five goals. I pushed off and glided toward centre on one foot, hoping I got to stay on Rasheed and Matthew's team.

I heard a deep, gravelly voice from the side of the rink say real loud, "Hey, Rasheed, I've seen enough." He added, "Why don't you introduce me to your new friend?"

Chapter 11

Rasheed pulled at my arm until I followed him to a man standing behind the fence. Undergrounders knew better than to trust adults, so I was totally on my guard.

"What's your name, son?" he asked.

"Jonathon."

"Well, Jonathon. That was some good stuff out there. You're a good skater. I love the creativity and puck control — you can't teach that. Rasheed told me you might come out this morning, and based on what he said I thought it would be worth taking the chance that you would play."

I got real nervous. Lewis had warned me about government people who threw street kids into juvie or foster care. Was that what was happening? The man didn't seem mean, and he smiled real big and looked friendly.

"I imagine you're wondering who I am. I'm Rasheed's hockey coach. My mom calls me Luigi — everyone else calls me Lou. Anyway, one of our forwards got hurt recently. Broke his leg snowboarding of all things, and we're a man down." He pressed his lips together real tight and grabbed hold of the fencing. "I understand you're not signed with anyone?"

I looked at Rasheed for help.

"He's not, Lou," Rasheed said.

"Tremendous." He scrunched his mouth to one side. "You're not the biggest kid I've seen. How tall are you?"

"Don't really know," I muttered. Like I need to be reminded I'm small.

"With your speed that shouldn't be a problem . . ." He rubbed his chin with his hand. "Do you mind taking a few shots on net?"

"Hey Collin, pass some pucks over, will ya?" Rasheed yelled.

"Sure thing," Collin answered.

A bunch of pucks came firing over. I felt dumb lining up at the blue line while everyone else stopped playing to watch. I didn't want to let Rasheed down, so I really laid into them and blasted a couple just under the crossbar. Another dinged off the post. I thought I did okay. The guys tapped their sticks on the ice, anyway.

"Come on over," Lou called to me.

"Do you go by Jonathon, or Jon, or Jonny?" Lou asked.

"Don't really care."

"I'll go with Jonny — a good hockey name. When I was younger I loved a player named Johnny Bucyk on the Bruins. Don't suppose you . . . Well, probably not, since you weren't even born when he retired." He cleared his throat. "Jonny, I'd like to invite you to our next practice. Have a skate with us and if you like it then maybe you can help us out for the rest of the season."

"And we could use the help," Collin quipped.

Lou laughed. "You boys are better than your record. I keep telling you that. We'll start winning." He looked at me. "Whaddaya say, Jonny?"

I would have given anything to say yes. It was impossible, of course. Undergrounders don't play hockey. It was dumb to even think about it. Besides, I didn't have equipment, and after what Lewis went through, I was done stealing. I figured the equipment angle was the nicest way to say no.

"I'd like to. Thanks for asking. But I don't have equipment and . . ."

"That's no problem," Lou practically exploded, laughing and slapping his thigh. "The sponsor provides the pants and helmet, and I put three boys and a daughter through hockey. I got enough gear at home to dress ten teams. You need shoulder, elbow and shin pads, right?"

I felt dizzy.

"How about a jock strap. Some boys are particular about using someone else's. Is that a big deal for you?"

I shook my head slightly.

"Tremendous. I'll see you there Tuesday night. Practice is at Win Hadley Memorial Arena at eight. Do you need a lift?"

This was insane!

"We can drive him," Rasheed said.

"Tremendous again. Looking forward to seeing

you, Jonny." He waved and began walking away. "Have fun, boys!"

"This is great," Rasheed said to me. "Where do you live and we'll pick you up."

"Are we gonna play some hockey?" Derrick said. "Hurry up, you two."

"Hold your horses," Rasheed said.

I figured the best thing was to agree and just not show up. "My house is kinda far away. Why don't I meet you here?"

"My dad won't mind picking you up. Are you sure?"

"Positive. I hang at my uncle's a lot . . . after school."

I was getting to be a fairly pro liar.

"We'll meet you here at seven, then."

"Come on, sticks in the middle," Collin said. "This time I'm playing with Jonathon," he said.

My head was really spinning. I'd actually been invited to try out for a real hockey team. I knew I couldn't play, but it was fun just to think about doing something other than hawking for change at the Market and dealing with Fitzy and Will — and just about everyone at the Underground.

I got my stick and followed Collin to the other end. I decided not to think about it until the game was over.

The puck squirted to the boards and I raced over to get it.

Chapter 12

Will stuffed himself into his sleeping bag and forced his way in between me and Rose. I pulled my sleeping bag up to my chest — it was too small to go higher — and I shook my shoulders as hard as I could. The cold in my body wouldn't go away.

"Stop shaking, Mouse," Will said. "You're so bloody annoying."

I was too cold to care. Rigger had let us in an hour early, and we were all crowded together in our store to try to stay warm. It had been brutal today. Even Reggies weren't going outside, and I hadn't hawked a cent.

"I can't feel my feet," J.J. whimpered for like the hundredth time and he rubbed them together.

"Quit squirming!" Will yelled.

"Could you stop spazzing out?" Rose said. "You're more irritating than the both of them put together."

"You're the spaz," Will shot back, and he pulled his sleeping bag over his head.

"So lame . . . so lame," Rose said. She rolled over on her side.

It got quiet again, and naturally I thought about the practice tonight. I'd obsessed over it all day: should I or shouldn't I? I'd even sharpened my skates again. Every time I convinced myself not to go, I'd think about it again. The shinny game had been so fun. To be able to play hockey for real would be too awesome.

Will lowered his blanket. "If you kick me again I'm gonna pound you, J.J."

J.J. was crying — as usual.

"Congratulations, jerk," Rose said. "If you're so tough why don't you kick an executive out of his store."

Will pulled his blankets over his head, but not before kicking J.J. with his boots. J.J. whimpered and moved over.

I couldn't take it. I had to leave. "I'm gonna go see if Lewis is back," I said, jumping to my feet.

"He ain't there," Rose said. "I just walked by his store."

My legs were stiff and it hurt to stand. My feet were tingling too. "Whatever. I'm not going to lie here all night and freeze to death."

"So what's the plan, Mouse? You going to a hotel?" Rose mocked.

"I'm going to play hockey."

I didn't mean to say it. It just came out.

Rose sat up. "You think it's smart to go outside? I know you like hockey, but that's downright stupid."

"I got asked to play, so I'm going to."

Will's head popped out from under his blankets. "Goody-goody for you," he said.

"Who are you playing with?" Rose pressed.

"Some guys I met at the rink."

"You've been playing hockey with Reggies?" Will said.

"Not good," Rose said. "They'll turn on you, trust me. I've seen it a million times. They don't put up with street kids — or anyone who ain't like them."

Since when did Rose look out for me?

"They aren't like that. They invited me to practice tonight — no big deal."

"You're dumber than I thought," Rose said, and with that she rolled on her side away from me.

I left. *She* was dumb. They all were. She was right about Lewis, though. He wasn't in; and that couch looked crazy comfortable. But I couldn't go in without permission; he'd kill me. Rigger was camped out on his chair, and he's the last guy I wanted to talk to. I put my head down and walked by.

"It's a thousand degrees below zero out there, Mouse. Where're you off to?"

"I'm playing hockey."

"What? Are you nuts?"

"It's not outside. I'm not stupid."

He grinned real big and flicked his eyebrows a couple times at me. "Don't forget us Undergrounders when you're in the NHL."

I grinned. "I'll get you a front-row seat."

"How about a private box?" he called out, as I started to climb up.

o o o

As I waited at the rink, there were moments I almost started whimpering like J.J. My feet were frozen, and I couldn't feel my hands either. I had to get my equipment from my hiding place, and then walk to the rink, and I almost quit a few times, but freezing to death was better than huddling in the Underground listening to J.J. snivelling and Rose and Will being idiots.

A blue van stopped in front of me and the side door flew open.

"Sorry we're late, Jonathon," Rasheed said. He seemed embarrassed. "I promised to clean my room and sorta forgot. Mom made me finish."

"I just got here myself."

"Well, get in. It's freezing."

"Open the trunk for him," the driver ordered.

"Sorry, Dad," Rasheed said. He hopped out and took my bag and stick without asking and tossed them into the back. He looked at me kind of strange and said, "Go on in."

The van was incredibly warm, like a furnace. Every part of my body relaxed, and I swear I could have laid down on the floor and gone to sleep right then and there. But his dad jolted me awake with a question, which I should have expected because adults are always firing questions at kids.

"So what school do you go to?" he asked me.

Every Undergrounder had an answer to that question in case a cop or some nosy do-gooder Reggie hassled you.

"I go to Glenwood, sir."

He laughed. "That's not far from the train station, right? And you can call me Rick, although I appreciate the manners."

Suddenly I smelled food. Rasheed was eating a sandwich — tuna. I hadn't eaten today. Money was too tight.

"Where did you move from?" Rick asked.

The smell made my head swim, like when you're sick and you feel all floaty.

"Jonathon, I was asking where did you move from?"

Luckily I had to cough, and I added a few more to give me time to think. "We lived in Brentwood, sir . . . I mean Rick."

"So not so far away. We went camping near there two summers ago. Remember, Rasheed?"

"Wasn't that the place with the rocky beach?"

Rick grunted. "I think you need to forgive me for that already."

Rasheed laughed. "Never. Too much fun bugging you about it." He pulled on my sleeve. "Lamest holiday ever. The beach was full of rocks and the water was ice-cold. We didn't go swimming the whole week."

"Are you eating, Rasheed?" Rick said. He didn't sound mad, though. "You have to eat something before practice."

Rasheed stuffed the sandwich into the bag. "Mom knows I hate tuna. I'm not hungry, anyway. And besides, we can get burgers at Johnny's after." He pulled on my sleeve again. "Have you been there?" I shook my head. "Best burger place in the world. We gotta take Jonathon to Johnny's, Dad."

He laughed. "We will, but not tonight. At least eat your banana."

"Do you like tuna?" he asked me.

"Sure."

I might have said that a bit too loud. A soggy piece of bread would have been okay, let alone a sandwich.

I couldn't slow down and probably looked like a massive pig. The sandwich disappeared big-time fast. Rick and Rasheed talked about the team while I ate. The Rangers had been together for three years, but after last season four of their best players, including Matthew, had left to play for the Red Wings.

I felt something poke me in the ribs. Rasheed put his finger to his lips and tossed a banana onto my lap. I polished that off and gave him the peel, which he held up so his dad could see it in the rear-view mirror.

"I finished the banana," Rasheed said to his dad. "What should I do with this?"

"We'll get rid of it at the rink. We should be there in ten minutes," Rick said.

"Can you turn on some tunes?" Rasheed asked.

I leaned back. My hands were getting their feeling back. I wished I could have said the same for my feet. They weren't going to thaw out for a while, for sure. Still, I wasn't complaining. I was fed and mostly warm. I closed my eyes and listened to the music.

○ ○ ○

My heart started racing. Where was I?

"Jonathon. Jonathon. Long day at the office?"

The voice seemed to come from far away.

"Practice time."

Someone was shaking me — Rasheed. I snapped out of my fog and remembered where I was, then stumbled out of the van behind him. Rick was holding my bag and stick out to me. I was so embarrassed I couldn't look at him when I took my stuff. Falling asleep — what a doofus move. Rasheed must be thinking I was the biggest loser.

I followed Rick and Rasheed to the rink, my nerves getting worse with practically every step. I couldn't believe this was really happening. This was crazy, going to a hockey practice, as if I were a normal, everyday kid, as if I had a home, parents, school, friends.

But to be honest, I wanted to make this team more than anything. I couldn't imagine my life without it, going back to the Underground and admitting I didn't make it to Will and Rose, so they could rub it in my face. I steeled myself as we went into the dressing room.

"Tremendous. You came," Lou said to me. "I have some equipment for you to try on."

Chapter 13

I was totally wiped out. Lou had seemed so laid back the first time I'd met him. Now he was a certifiable maniac, making us skate in circles, backward and forward and sideways and jumping. My legs were limp as spaghetti when he blew his whistle and waved us to the bench. I was a little irritated that I was the only one who seemed out of breath.

"I want to work on our power play a bit," Lou said. "Give me Rasheed, Jacob and Derrick up front, with Collin and Peter on D." He looked around and his eyes settled on me. "Penalty killers will be Michael and . . . Jonny as forwards, and Simon and Carlos on defence. Andrew can start in net for the power play; Nicholas, you be on the kill. The rest of you go on the bench for now."

The other players scampered off the ice. "We're having a ton of trouble breaking out of our end and getting into the neutral zone with speed," Lou said to us. "We'll go the whole ice; the team with the man advantage has the puck."

Rasheed and his linemates skated to the far end. Lou tugged on my sweater and pointed at the whiteboard with a marker.

"Here's our penalty-killing system. One man deep, and he forces the play left or right. Second man stays at the blue line and looks to intercept a pass or force the play to the outside. If the puck gets past you, hustle back and set up the box. Got it?"

I nodded — but I most definitely did not get it. I knew the box meant the four penalty killers formed a box in our end in front of our goalie. Ron was a creep, but he knew a lot about hockey and he taught me stuff when we watched games on TV. I also remembered a few things my coaches told me. But we never had any systems. We just went after the puck.

Michael glided over. "I'll be first in. You take the left point in our end." He didn't wait for an answer, and skated off.

Lou shot the puck down the right wall, and Michael took off after it. I followed, not too sure exactly where to go. Lou told me to anticipate the pass. Peter had it behind his net. Jacob didn't look that eager, and I knew Derrick loved to carry it. I gambled on him and cheated his way. Then like a total doofus Peter passes it, and I'm right there to pick it off. I'm laughing it was so easy. Andrew came out to challenge, but I figured the short side up high was open — the puck banged off the post and in.

Lou blasted his whistle. He didn't look too happy. "That was good . . . Michael, Jonny." He pointed at

Peter. "Maybe not so good on the breakout. Can we try again?"

Andrew shovelled the puck to Peter, and I drifted backward to the blue line. This time Derrick circled behind the net and scooped up the puck. Michael cut left to head him off. Since Jacob was a pylon, I didn't worry about him. For sure Derrick would drop it to Peter, and right on cue when Michael got near, Derrick dropped it. If Peter then passed it across to Jacob I'd have been beat for sure, but he tried to deke and I stripped him of the puck, beat the goalie on a backhand deke, and flipped it into the left corner.

Lou blasted his whistle — he loved that thing — and he looked real grumpy. "Which side's got the power play?" Peter banged his stick on the ice, which made me feel kind of good. I'd burned him twice already.

Lou snapped his fingers. "I've got an idea," he said with a sour face. "Let's have Jonny on D this time. Peter, take a break.."

Peter stared at Lou, real unhappy. "I'll get it next time," he said. "The puck hit his skate by accident. I've got it figured out."

"I just want to try it once," Lou said. "No big deal. Have a seat on the bench and I'll get you back in."

Peter had a bit of a hissy fit, which reminded me of J.J. Lou gave me the puck. "Start behind the net. Skate with it until you feel pressure, then pass it to an open wing. If you get it in the offensive zone, look to Collin for the big slapper." He turned to the bench. "Daniel, take Jonny's place on the kill."

I took the puck behind the net like he told me and came out the right side. Michael charged me, but I expected that and switched it inside and got past him. That Daniel kid covered Derrick, so I kept going. Rasheed drifted wide right. The defenceman, Simon, had one hand on the stick and the other up in the air like he was answering a question or something. I dangled the puck behind me, head-faked to the inside, then bounced outside. I'd practised that ten thousand times at the rink and it was second nature. Simon fell for the inside move and I was in alone.

Nicholas came way out. Was he crazy? That made it easy for me. I took it hard to my backhand and stuffed it in before he could jam his pad against the post.

Lou waved me over. He still didn't look happy. "You forced your wingers to hold up at the blue line, and I think Derrick was offside on that goal. Pass once you get open, or get to the red line and dump it into the corner."

Wasn't the point of the game to score?

"So I shouldn't carry it in by myself?"

"Not all the time. We need to work on our passing too." He slapped my shoulder. "But as the kids say, that was sweet."

That made me feel better.

"Let's try it again," Lou shouted.

I was happy to. This was more fun than eating a hot dog at the station, than ten Chinese buns, even more fun than hanging with Lewis on the couch. This was real hockey, with other kids, in an indoor arena. I could have played forever.

o o o

After the practice ended two other adults, the assistant coaches, began collecting the pucks, and all the players headed off the ice. I looked for a loose puck to take a few more shots. I didn't want this to end. We'd gone over the power play a few more times — and I did pretty good. Rasheed and I scored a few times, and Collin blasted in two from the point off my passes.

"Hey, Jonathon. Like, how many did you score?"

Collin and Rasheed skated over.

"I dunno. A couple, I guess."

"A couple," Collin snorted. "I think a couple hundred is more like it." He put his arm around my neck. "I can't believe how a little guy like you can skate with the puck all the time and never get hit — and that shot! You got a cannon, harder than mine, and I'm way bigger."

Rasheed squeezed my arm. "Small but strong. Check out these pipes."

That probably came from climbing the ladder in and out of the Underground.

"Can I talk to you for a second?" Lou called out to me.

I joined him at the boards. The two other adults were there also.

"This is Ian and Malcolm," Lou said. "They're the assistant coaches. We all liked what we saw."

"Maybe we need to work on some positioning and passing," Malcolm added.

"And we love that shot," Ian said.

"I confess I was worried about the size factor," Lou said. "You skate like the wind and always keep your head up." He rubbed his chin with his hand. "So do you think you're up for it?"

"Up for what?"

Lou laughed. "Up for joining the Rangers. We'd love to have you play for the rest of the season."

"We just have to work out something for the fee," Malcolm said.

I hated that Malcolm. Of course, they'd charge me to play. I was so dense sometimes.

"Maybe your parents can call us," Malcolm continued.

Not likely!

"Is that going to be a problem?" Lou asked quietly.

More like impossible. "My uncle just bought me skates, and a stick, and gloves. I don't think I can ask him for more; and my mom doesn't have . . . she won't be able to . . . she told me that . . ."

The coaches were just looking at me.

"Thanks for the equipment and everything. I'll leave it in the dressing room," I said.

"Hold on, son," Lou said. "I hate to think a boy with your natural talent can't play because of money — hockey's too expensive as it is." He waved his hand. "Forget the fee. We have enough money for this year."

He held out his hand. "Welcome to the Rangers." I couldn't believe it. I shook his hand, and then shook with Ian and Malcolm, although I noticed Malcolm snuck a look at Lou that I knew meant he wasn't happy about the money. But Lou was the boss, so I didn't care. The Rangers — this was over the top.

"Head on in and we'll announce it to the team," Lou said.

So off we went to the dressing room. I heard Rasheed laughing as Lou pushed the door open.

"I never miss," Rasheed was saying. Collin's mouth was wide open and Rasheed was about to let fly with a tape ball.

"Hold it down to a dull roar," Lou said. "And you can drop the tape, Rasheed."

Rasheed laughed and threw the tape into a garbage can.

"Swish! A trey," Rasheed said, holding his arms over his head.

"Jonny has agreed to join the Rangers family in place of Brandon," Lou announced.

The room went real quiet, which kind of worried me. Rasheed clapped and said, "Awesome," and Collin said, "That's great, coach." Everyone else just sat there. Peter and Jacob were obviously mad. Derrick didn't look too stoked either. It was hard to tell about the others.

Lou clapped me on the shoulder. "I'll need you to sign some forms, and also for your parents to sign the insurance waiver. Get changed and I'll get them for you from the car."

I was too stunned to answer. It all happened so fast. I'd actually made a hockey team, like a regular kid. I was a Reggie!

I sat next to Rasheed, and Collin came over.

"This is seriously cool, dude," Collin said. "With you we might actually win a game."

Rasheed and Collin high-fived. I took off my helmet and started to untie my skates, trying hard to keep calm. I felt like jumping up and down and screaming like crazy, because I was so stoked.

If those loser Undergrounders could see me now!

Chapter 14

I coughed until I thought my eyes were going to pop out of my head. That stupid Rose must have made me sick. My cough sounded like hers. J.J. had it too. Last night Will threw a total fit because we all couldn't stop coughing.

"This spot sucks eggs," J.J. said, hugging himself around the chest and rubbing his sides with his hands. "How much have you hawked?"

I dug out some change. J.J. snorted. "A dollar! Great. I only got fifty cents. What are we gonna buy for that?"

I knew he was lying because I was lying too. I'd hidden another dollar in my sock.

"Not our fault. It's too cold to hawk. The Reggies aren't walkin' around."

"Let's try near the TV station," he suggested.

"Will said to wait here," I said.

"Will Schmill," J.J. sneered. He was always talking tough when people weren't around. "This is dumb. Come on."

But I wanted to hang around because I had a hockey game tonight and 1 needed to get my equipment. Besides, Will and Rose were hawking at the subway station and we were going to pool our money for food, which I could use because my money was getting low and I'd skipped eating this morning.

"Let's wait another minute," I offered.

"Don't be dumb. I want to go. This is lame."

"What's so great about the TV station? It's way lamer."

"You're being lame. You afraid to go there or something?"

"That's dumb. I've been there like a thousand times."

J.J. shrugged. "Then a thousand and one won't kill you." He turned and headed down the street.

No way I'd let myself look like a weenie to J.J. He'd tell everyone that I was too scared. I've got to admit that I was nervous about it. A lot of Streeters hung out there. I'd heard about fights breaking out and worse — not good for a guy whose nickname is Mouse.

And sure enough a pile of Streeters were in front. The station had huge windows so you could look in from the sidewalk. Sometimes they even had rock stars inside performing, or so Lewis told me.

"We shouldn't bother," I tried one last time. "There's too much competition to hawk here."

"I wanna see the studio," J.J. insisted.

He is such an idiot.

"We won't make any money. There's like ten Streeters and they all . . ."

"Forget you. I'm gonna look."

I really wanted to brain the guy. He was so stubborn, although I admit he didn't seem scared. J.J. slipped past some Streeters I didn't recognize and pushed his way to the front, and practically pressed his nose into the glass. I couldn't have cared less and stayed back. I needed money more than to see some doofus rock star. I needed the rent and I wanted a Chinese bun, and if I could swing it I was totally in the mood for a Coke.

The next second I was sprawled out on the sidewalk and looking up at a big hunk of nasty named W5.

"If it ain't Lewis's little doggie."

Why would W5 be after me? Yesterday I'd dropped a package off and everything was fine. I sat up.

"What's the deal?" I said, rubbing my back.

He kneeled down and grabbed me by the shirt. "Tell that puke Lewis that he owes me fifty bucks, and I'd better get it soon or he'll be dead. I mean it."

The two jerks next to him thought that was hilarious. I picked myself off the ground, went over and pulled on J.J.'s sleeve. "We gotta go. No action here. Will's waiting for us."

He kept his stupid face pressed up against the window. "Chill. There's a show on."

"We're going," I hissed, pulling his arm. I was so mad at him I swear my head was going to explode.

"Let go, you freakin' . . . What're ya doing?"

The loser put up such a fuss everyone was looking — not good.

"I don't think he wants to dance with you," W5 said real loud.

That got a big laugh, of course. I let J.J. go. "I'm leaving," I whispered.

A big hand closed on my shoulder and a thumb dug under my collarbone. It hurt so bad I was paralysed by the pain.

It was W5. "Why so eager?" He eyed me real close. "I bet you're loaded."

My heart was about to jump out of my chest.

"Let's see what you got in your pockets," he growled, and slapped me kind of hard across the face.

"I . . . I . . . don't have anything," I managed.

"Prove it."

He let me go, but now his friends had me sur-rounded — no escape. And then out of the corner of my eye, what do I see but J.J. crossing the street. Stupid jerk.

"Start with the right pocket," Scrunchy Face ordered. His hair was greasier than usual. I pulled the pocket out. "Now the other one," he said.

This time the loonie fell out, and Scrunchy Face picked it up. "I thought you didn't have nothin'," he snarled. His breath smelled gross, like fried chicken. "I bet he's got more. Let me work him over and find out." He pulled me by my collar.

"I don't have more, I swear. I gotta go meet some-one. I gotta . . . I gotta . . ."

"I gotta. I gotta," W5 mimicked in a high-pitched voice.

Scrunchy Face threw me to the ground. "You look scared," he said. "Is it 'cause you're about to get pounded?"

Lewis had taught me what to do in a street fight. Get the first shot in, and hit him where it hurts. Then run like the wind. I got to my feet.

"Should I start with your face, or loosen you up with a couple of body shots?"

"Start with this," I yelled, and smashed him right in the crown jewels. I didn't wait for more questions. I sprinted across the street, and kept going even though I heard car tires screeching.

"You're dead, dude. Dead!"

I didn't dare look back. J.J. was such a traitor! They were going to kill me for sure, especially if they found the loonie in my sock. Where should I go? They'd get me soon. Big kids are fast. The only thing I could think of was the Theatre. Maybe Will or Rose would be there, not that they could do much against W5.

I turned the corner and snuck a look. W5 was catching up. I kept running, dodging Reggies the whole way. No one gave me a second look; who was going to help a street kid? My legs hurt and so did my shoulder where W5 grabbed me. I'd be hurt a lot more when he caught me.

"No chance, puke. Stop or I'll punish you worse."

I came to a red light but I didn't stop for a second. A big truck came barrelling down the street and W5 had to wait, which let me turn the corner again and get a lead. I turned down a small street behind the Theatre.

Up ahead was the garbage bin. Something crazy came to me. I looked back and they hadn't turned down the alley yet. Without thinking I jumped up and rolled into the bin, pulling some bags over my head, praying he hadn't seen me. The smell was unreal — rotten eggs mixed with vomit, I swear. But that was nothing compared with the torture of waiting for him to find me.

I forced myself not to make a sound — not to move a muscle — not to even breathe — so I held my breath for as long as I could before taking another one real quiet. Try doing that when you have a cough. I thought my lungs were going to burst.

I heard someone run by but couldn't be sure it was him. At least the garbage was soft. Maybe it was from a restaurant, because I know there's one in the Theatre. I counted to a hundred three times, and then slowly peeked out the top of the bin.

I took my first deep breath; the coast was clear. I pushed the garbage bags off, and then slumped back down. This is great, I thought: sitting in garbage, the nastiest Streeter in the world after me, J.J. runs off, I smell like crap, and I have my first hockey game tonight with the Rangers. Maybe because no one was around, but for whatever reason a tear snuck out of my eye, and after that I couldn't stop. Why couldn't I just play hockey all the time? On the ice, I didn't think about the Underground or Streeters, or always being hungry, or living with idiots who bugged me, or missing my mom so much I got a sick feeling in my stomach.

Thank God the tears finally ran out. What really

sucked was I'd lost my extra dollar to W5 and couldn't buy a Coke unless I hawked some more cash. Fat chance of that, smelling like this, and I felt my butt was all wet from something — now that was gross.

Stupid J.J.

Chapter 15

"Mouse. Where have you been? I'm tired of waiting. J.J. said you were right behind him."

Will glared at me with his hands on his hips. Rose looked at me with her nose all pulled back like she couldn't understand something. J.J. slunk off to the side.

"I had some W5 problems to deal with," I said, real calm.

All of a sudden Will didn't look like he wanted to pound me.

"You got blood on your coat," Rose said.

"Did you fight W5?" Will said, his eyes wide.

"That loser took my money. But I popped one guy in the crown jewels and took off."

"Yeah, right," Will said, waving me off.

"It's true," J.J. said. "W5 whacked him in the face a few times and then this tall, skinny guy was gonna pound him. Jonathon punched him good. I saw it."

Will actually laughed. "You surprise me sometimes, Mouse. I wish I could've seen it. Just thinking about it is worth a bun, anyway. Come with us, and I'll buy you one."

"Okay. Thanks. It was a good shot too. The loser fell right to the pavement."

"Too bad it wasn't W5," Will growled. "Do that to him and I'll buy you a hot dog." He pointed down the street and walked off.

"You got some blood on your face too," Rose said as she passed me.

I licked my fingers and rubbed my face to get it off. The taste was salty and beefy, and it nearly made me sick. J.J. kept away from me the whole way to Winston's. I figured the best thing was to say nothing and let him stew. I guess there wasn't anything he could have done to help me, and he did back me up in front of Will and Rose. Still, I wasn't going to be nice; he didn't deserve it.

The sun was going down. Rigger could tell me the time. I hoped I had a chance to rest before the game. I had to meet Rasheed at his house by six thirty, and since I was so low on cash I couldn't take the subway. I could have eaten ten Chinese buns, I was so starved.

We got our buns and went back to the Underground. Creeper was guarding the door. He nodded at me. "What happened to you? Run into a truck?"

J.J. answered for me. "W5 pounded on him. Stole his coin too. Mouse punched one of W5's crew in the nuts and got away."

Creeper whistled softly. "Mouse the enforcer. Didn't figure you for a scrapper."

He didn't say it in his usual mean way. Maybe this fight would be a good thing, make me more legit to the Undergrounders. Everyone seemed impressed, even Will.

"That loser fell like a sack of potatoes. You shoulda seen it," I bragged.

"That's a rough crew," Creeper said seriously. "Have you told Lewis yet?"

That's when it hit me. How could I make deliveries to W5 for Lewis? This was serious bad.

I shrugged as if I didn't care. "I ain't afraid of them. I'll do what I want."

"You comin'?" J.J. said, his foot on the ladder.

"Yeah. Yeah. Quit buggin' me. Go ahead," I snapped, and J.J. started climbing down. Creeper was looking out the window. "I'll see ya, Creeper," I said to him. He didn't turn around or answer, so I followed J.J. The climb hurt like anything with my hurt shoulder. I'd also jammed my wrist when I jumped into the bin. I ignored it and kept going, hopping down the last couple of rungs the way all the legit Undergrounders do. I prayed it was only five o'clock so I could relax a bit and clean up, or the guys would think I was a freak.

J.J., Rose and Will were waiting for me.

"Can you ask Lewis for his cards?" J.J. asked. "We wanna play Crazy Eights."

"I'll ask him — but I can't play," I said.

"Why not?" J.J. demanded.

After what happened I didn't figure I had to answer to him. I started off to Rigger. Will wasn't so easy to ignore. He grabbed my arm.

"Our Mouse is all fired up after his W5 experience. Don't you be disrespecting me or getting ideas," he said.

I felt like giving *him* a shot to the crown jewels. Nowhere to run, though. "I'm going out later, so I don't have time."

"We can play until you go," J.J. said.

Suddenly, we were best freakin' friends. To shut them up I decided to come clean. "I have a hockey game tonight, and I can't be late."

Will burst out laughing — not exactly the reaction I'd expected. Rose yawned. "You actually made that hockey team?" she asked.

"I'm playing for a AA team, for your information," I said, and stomped off.

"Hey, Rigger. What time you got?"

He stretched out in his chair and slowly raised his arm. "Five thirty, my little Mouse."

I groaned. I had to leave in fifteen minutes.

"So what happened to your face?" he asked.

"Nothing," I said, and rushed to the washroom to clean up. The blood came off my coat pretty good, but my sweatshirt was stained. I had my backup one in my sleeping bag. It was ugly, but it was better than showing up smelling like garbage. I washed the dirty one as best I could. Hopefully, it would dry by tomorrow. I was going to have to change into my other pants too, which was not good because I had worn them all last week and they were still dirty. I had to scrub real hard to get the dried blood off my face. It was all I could do to keep my eyes open, so the cold water felt good in a shocking way.

Halfway up the ladder my shoulder started to burn like it was on fire, and my wrist was all achy. I stopped three times, and usually I didn't stop at all.

Creeper peered down at me. "What ya doing, Mouse?"

Speaking would take too much energy. I had ten rungs to go. One at a time, I told myself.

"Hurry up, Mouse. You having a baby?"

I scrambled up the last few rungs.

"What's the deal? Did you forget something?"

"Nah. I . . . um . . . I got a hockey game."

"Give me a break. How's that?"

"I was asked to play . . . on this team . . . the Rangers."

Creeper whistled. "That's crazy stuff, Mouse. An Undergrounder playing hockey. What's next? You going to go to school?"

"Nothing that crazy." I wanted to get going. I still had to pick up my stuff from my hiding place behind the Theatre.

But Creeper seemed to have a million questions like everyone else. "So where do you play?"

"Not sure exactly where. I'm meeting up with some guys on the team near the outdoor rink at Cedarview Park."

"Long walk — and it's cold tonight. You should take the subway."

"Yeah, right. W5 took all my money."

Creeper nodded slowly and reached into his pocket.

"Take this," he said.

It was a ticket for the subway. Why would a guy like him do that? It was nice all the same, and suddenly I felt like using his real name, but all I knew was Creeper. "That's awesome. Thanks."

"I played a little when I was . . . your age. I was pretty good too. You can take it off the money I owe you."

We looked at each other. "Well, thanks again. I better get going."

"You go for it, Mouse. Score one for me tonight."

I flashed a thumbs up and opened the door.

"Remember, the drawbridge locks at eleven o'clock tonight. Don't be late."

"No problem. Game starts at seven thirty."

I stuffed the ticket into my pocket and headed to the subway, the hard snow crunching underfoot as I ran.

Chapter 16

Lou slapped his clipboard against his hand a few times and the guys quieted down.

"Now that's more like it," he said. Lou was all red in the face and laughing and happy; all the Rangers were. Rasheed and Collin probably high-fived like a hundred times, and the parents had crowded the dressing-room door and clapped us in. They'd gone nuts when the game ended.

"The monkey's most definitely off our backs. See what happens when you work hard and commit to the system? Not to mention four power-play goals."

The guys let out a big cheer.

"Three of them by Jonathon," Rasheed yelled.

Collin reached over and I high-fived him. I had to use my left hand because my wrist was really aching. My shoulder hurt too. Stickhandling hadn't been too bad, but shooting was painful.

I noticed Peter whispering to Jacob. They weren't cheering along with the others. Lou had put me back on the point for the power play in Peter's place, and he'd taken Jacob off Rasheed's line for me.

"Great win, Rangers," Lou continued. "I can hardly wait for the next game. We practise on Thursday, so enjoy the victory and let's see if we can build on it.'

The coaches left, and I began to get undressed. But first I had to cough about ten times.

Collin slapped my shin pads with a stick. "So, J-Man. Four goals in your first game — you're practically our leading scorer already."

All of a sudden I felt weird in my head, like I was floating and looking at myself, and there was this empty feeling in my stomach.

"What d'ya say, J-Man," Collin said. "Big win, or what?"

The room was quiet, and it dawned on me that all the guys were looking. The room smelled so bad, like dirty socks, even worse than the Underground, which is saying a lot.

Rasheed leaned forward. "You okay, Jonathon?"

Why was it so hot? "I'm good," I managed. "That was fun. Good game."

I had to leave: it was a furnace, and now there was a pounding in my head. "I'll wait for you outside." I got up to go.

"Did you come in your equipment?" Peter said, laughing at me. "This ain't house league."

I was still wearing my pants and shin pads. I hated that jerk. A wave of hunger hit me. It wasn't so bad during the game. I could have eaten my right hand now. Quick as I could, I ripped off my equipment, stuffed it into my bag, and without a word charged out.

I must have looked like a freak, but if I hadn't left I would have passed out for sure. The cold arena air cleared my head a bit and I headed for the lobby. How was I going to survive tonight? Maybe Lewis would have some bread. I'd never been so hungry in my life.

"Jonathon, that was a fine game. On that third goal, I think you deked out the entire team. Well done."

It was Rasheed's dad. And I couldn't believe it when he handed me a carton of chocolate milk.

"Best thing after a game," he said. "Replaces the sugars after exercise. Of course, once you get to a certain age . . ." He patted his stomach.

I inhaled it. I think he really saved my life — no kidding. I was that close to dying. I never tasted anything so good — ever.

"I see you like chocolate milk," Rick said dryly.

I kept forgetting Reggies were different, and they cared about manners and stuff. "Sorry. I didn't really have time for dinner and I was . . . thirsty."

He laughed. "After that performance, you don't have to apologize for anything. And if you're hungry, let's go to Johnny's for burgers. We should celebrate the first win of the season."

A woman came over. "It's getting a bit late, honey. Maybe we should do it another day."

Johnny's was the burger place Rasheed loved. But I had no money.

"This is a big occasion," Rick said. "We'll be quick, I promise. Besides, I'm hungry too."

She took a deep breath. "Well . . . okay. I guess this is an important moment." She whispered to Rick, "I confess I didn't think we were going to win a game all year." She turned to a girl next to her. "Alisha, do you want to go with the boys to Johnny's?"

She rolled her eyes, as if her mom was wack for even asking.

"I'll take that as a yes," her mom said, laughing.

Her laugh was nice. She squeezed Rick's arm. "Try to get them back quickly. It is a school night."

"Let me introduce you to Jonathon," Rick said, "our new scoring machine."

She held out her hand and I shook it. If she only knew about the garbage bin, she wouldn't be doing that so quick.

"You certainly had a wonderful game," she said. "My goodness, how you can skate. I can only imagine how excited the boys are to do so well."

"They are . . . excited . . . to win, I guess, ma'am."

My mom taught me ladies like polite kids. Rasheed's mom burst out laughing, though.

"And good manners to go with his skills. What a charmer. Please call me Cynthia. It's great to meet you, Jonathon. I'll see you later, Rick."

Then came this killer awkward moment standing around with Rick and Alisha that felt like forever. Alisha looked at me a few times, but always turned away as if she'd done something wrong. I probably smelled like a garbage can, so I bet she was scared of me.

I was never so happy to see Rasheed and Collin.

Those guys take forever to get changed, and boy, are they loud. Next thing I know we're all in the van, including Collin, off to this Johnny's place. This was a nightmare. I had no money. I could not sit and watch them eat. It would be like torture. That chocolate milk was good, but I needed food.

I was a nervous wreck when we pulled into the parking lot at Johnny's. It was a nice-looking place — a real old-fashioned burger joint.

"You coming, Jonathon?"

Rasheed had slid open the van door.

"I guess. Sorry."

"You don't have anything to be sorry about," he said, closing the door behind me, "not the way you played today." He slapped me on the back. "This place is the best. You gotta get the double-burger — total automatic call. The shakes are just okay, but get one anyway. Fries — of course. I'm feeling all onion-ringy, though. What about you?"

I felt the two quarters in my pocket — my life savings. "I didn't know we were . . . coming here and I didn't . . . exactly bring enough . . ." My voice sounded all squeaky, like a little kid about to burst into tears. Rasheed was looking at me all funny. "I don't have any money," I said in a rush, and prayed I wouldn't start crying.

Rasheed laughed and slapped my back again. "Dad's got you covered. Don't sweat it. And this joint's named after you, so you shouldn't have to pay." He kept laughing as we went in. Alisha held the door for us. For the first time I noticed her bright green eyes, which stood out against her brown skin and long, straight black hair.

"Thanks," I mumbled, as I walked past.

"You're welcome," she said.

Those were the first words I heard her say. She was small, shorter than me, and I figured she'd have a high voice, but it was smoother and lower even than Rose's. She was way prettier than Rose too.

Chapter 17

Rasheed had his arm around Collin's shoulder. "I assume you're going for the double double-burger."

"As much as that appeals to me, good friend, I fear that would be somewhat expensive and therefore, out of respect for your father I will limit my appetite to one pathetic, barely-fills-me-up regular burger, with no toppings, no drink, and no fries — and perhaps get a snack when I go home."

Rick lowered his chin to his chest, but I could tell he thought it was funny. He peered over at the pair of them. "I think I might be able to finance the double double-burger on this tremendous occasion. You need to keep your energy up, considering the Rangers are on a winning streak."

"I won't let you down, Rick." Collin cleared his throat. "And I'll have the burgers with everything but tomatoes, and perhaps I'll add a large fries, chocolate shake — and maybe Rasheed and I can split some rings?"

Rick rolled his eyes. "To be young again. And Rasheed — the usual?"

"Sure, Dad. Make mine a banana shake."

"What do you want, Alisha?"

She crinkled her nose. Her eyes were really bright, and her skin was so smooth it glowed. I'd never seen skin like that. She sort of looked like Rasheed too, but in a girl way, of course.

"Hot dog and fries and a vanilla shake," she said.

Rick looked at me and raised his eyebrows. "I assume you want two double-burgers also."

The burger smell was so strong I could almost taste it, which made my mouth all watery and I had to gulp a ton of saliva. I prayed Alisha didn't notice.

Thank God Rasheed answered for me. "He's got double double-burger written all over his face."

I could have hugged him.

"*Doin' da double double ting,*" Collin chanted.

"Grab a table and I'll order," Rick said.

As I followed them, Rick called out, "Jonathon, I forgot. What do you want on your burgers?"

"Maybe ketchup, mustard . . . and pickles and onions . . . and hot peppers."

For some reason Rick thought that was funny, and I could tell because I know when adults try not to laugh. "And to drink?"

This was definitely over the top. "Chocolate shake, I guess."

Rasheed and Collin were sitting next to each other, so I had to sit beside Alisha. I hoped I didn't smell too bad. My knee touched hers by mistake and I moved away real fast so she wouldn't get mad. She smiled at me when I squeezed in, though, and I smiled back.

"I'm still so stoked by the game," Collin was saying. "I think Jonathon killed that whole penalty by himself in the first period."

We got a penalty and the puck just seemed to follow me around. I carried it in our end, then circled through the neutral zone and back into our end, and then all the way down to their end. I didn't score, but Lou still made a big fuss when I came off, and I killed every penalty after that.

"The third goal was the best," Rasheed said, "when you split the D and put it under the crossbar on your backhand. I mean, Jonathon, that was insane skill."

I wish they'd stop talking about me. It was embarrassing in front of Alisha.

All I could think of saying was, "I thought the team played good."

Rasheed and Collin began to laugh so loud the other customers began to look over. Alisha giggled too. Her laugh was musical, like she was singing a song, the opposite of Rose. Her laugh was like a soggy cough.

"You keep scoring and the team will play *really* good," Rasheed said.

He and Collin began talking about the next game against the Flames, who were in second place behind the Red Wings.

"What school do you go to?" I heard Alisha say.

It took me a few seconds to realize she was asking me. "I doubt you've heard of it. I don't live that close to you."

"Oh."

"Where do you go?" I asked.

She giggled again. "Same as Rasheed."

"What grade?"

She giggled even harder. "Same grade. We're twins, in case you didn't notice. We don't have any classes together, though."

Rasheed must have heard that. "We would if you didn't hang out with all those gifties."

"You'd be in the gifted program too if you did your homework and tried for once."

"I did my homework once — just can't remember when."

Alisha didn't look impressed — more like disgusted. "You're such a doofus, sometimes."

"Takes one to know one," Rasheed shot back.

"Food!" Collin interrupted.

Rick slid two trays onto the table. Rasheed and Collin reached out, only to have Alisha slap their hands away.

"Jonathon's the guest of honour today. You animals can wait. Go ahead, take yours," she said to me.

"I'm not sure which one is mine."

"I heard you ask for hot peppers, so they're probably the ones with HP written on them."

I took my two burgers. Collin and Rasheed were laughing and I could feel myself blush.

"Shut up, you two," she said, and took her hot dog. "You're both such goofs."

Rick sat down and handed out the drinks. "Let's eat up. It's getting late."

The first burger went down so fast I didn't remember eating it. Rasheed poured the fries and onion rings onto some napkins in the middle of the table and we dug in. It took all my energy not to scarf them all down myself.

I was halfway through my second burger when Rick ruined it all.

"We should get going," he said. "It's almost ten o'clock."

"Don't sweat it," Collin said. "My parents love it when I'm out."

They all laughed. I practically choked on my burger. I didn't know if I could get from the rink to the Theatre to drop off my equipment and then to the Underground before the door was locked. I'd have to sleep outside. My mind seemed to freeze even thinking about it. Maybe I could sleep on a vent, but the drunks would be there by now. I'd have to walk around all night to keep warm. I thought about the door next to the shopping mall. Maybe they hadn't fixed it yet and I could sneak into the stairway.

Alisha tugged on my arm. She must have noticed my reaction, because she asked if I was all right.

"My mom likes me home . . . on school nights. No problem. Didn't know it was so late."

No one else seemed that worried, not even Rick, so it took another ten minutes to finish. My burger tasted like chalk all of a sudden.

"Why don't we finish our milkshakes in the van," Rick said.

Rasheed sucked on his straw and it made that crackling noise that means you're done. "Not necessary, Dad. I've solved the problem."

Seconds later, Collin did the same, and then Alisha. They all looked at me. I sucked so hard on that straw I thought I'd puke. Finally, I heard that empty sound and slammed the cup down. I had to force myself not to scream, I was so mad. Everything was such a big joke to them.

Chapter 18

The clock in the van read 10:15 when we finally pulled out of the parking lot. I was totally messed in the head. Maybe the best plan was to sleep in the garbage bin and use the bags as blankets.

And then as if I wasn't stressed enough, Rick asked me where I lived. "Your house is by the train station, right?" he asked me.

I'd assumed he'd drop me off at the rink. "Um . . . yeah."

"What's the address?"

"You can drop me off at the rink. I'll walk home."

He laughed. "Don't be silly, Jonathon. It's ten thirty. I can't have you walking home across the city. Your mom would kill me." He paused. "So . . . your address?"

I remembered the row of townhouses behind the station. I had no idea of the street name, though. "It's right behind the station. Do you know the townhouses there? It's just on that street. You take Front to . . ."

"I know those places. They're nice. I remember

when they were built. Not a problem. It's not that out of the way, actually. We'll be there in ten minutes, tops."

The rest of the ride was pure agony. Rasheed and Collin joked the whole way. Did they ever shut up? It's great when you have a soft, warm bed to look forward to. I had a night of street walking. I'd probably get pounded by drunks or freeze to death. I complained about the Underground all the time, but I tell you, now that I was going to be locked out I'd have given anything to get in there.

It felt like it took forever before we turned onto the street where I supposedly lived.

"What number is it?" Rick asked.

I picked a house with the lights off. "The one next to the stop sign."

He pulled the van over. The clock read 10:45. Rasheed hopped out and opened the trunk.

"Thanks for the lift," I said, "and Johnny's."

"Great game, Jonathon," Rasheed said. "Do you need a lift to the practice on Wednesday? We can give him a lift, right Dad?"

"Sure. It's early, at seven thirty. Is it possible for you to meet us at our house again? We'll have to leave at six thirty sharp."

"That's fine," I said. I wasn't really thinking about practice. I could feel the wind right through my jacket.

"See ya," Rasheed said, and he got back in.

"Nice to meet you," Alisha said, as the door closed.

I waved at her and went to the trunk to get my equipment and stick. As I did, I noticed a blue nylon

111

bag with a pull string. I reached over and pulled it a bit — a sleeping bag! Most Undergrounders would kill for a real sleeping bag. Mine was barely better than a bed sheet; it was so short I had to sleep all crunched up, and the bottom was beginning to tear. I snatched it and stuffed it in my hockey bag as fast as I could.

"Hey, Jonathon." Rasheed was leaning over the back seat grinning at me. "You were on fire tonight. For the first time all season I'm actually looking forward to the next game. See ya Wednesday."

I was too scared to answer. Would he notice the sleeping bag?

"So . . . I'll see ya," he repeated.

"Okay. Bye," I managed finally.

I waved, but the van did not move. Then I realized they were waiting for me to go inside. I looked around and saw a gate leading to the backyard. I pulled on the latch and waved again. That convinced them this was my house and the van pulled away. I kept waving until they were out of sight. It was snowing lightly and the streets were quiet. The street was actually real pretty, with these old-fashioned street lights and all the houses looking the same. If only I was actually going inside a house, life would be perfect. I closed the gate and headed down the street.

I didn't have time to drag this hockey bag all the way to the Theatre. I decided to stash it inside the door to the Underground. Rigger would charge me extra if he knew, but I could get up early and move it before he found out. Hopefully, Creeper was still guarding and he wouldn't squeal. He hated Rigger more than anyone. At least I wasn't hungry, and the game had been fun. I hadn't thought about food, or Will, or W5, or anything for the entire time we played. I wished the game had gone on forever — that I could just play hockey and not have to worry about anything.

I skidded down the hill, trying not to fall with the hockey bag on my shoulder. I used my stick to balance me, and I made it. In the window by the door, I thought I saw something flash, like a light. I held my breath as I sprinted to the door. Rigger had warned us about banging on the drawbridge after curfew, so I lightly tapped a few times with my stick.

Creeper peered out with a cigarette hanging between his lips. I'd never thought I would be happy to see him.

"You're lucky I decided to have a smoke before going down," he said.

I'd never been happier to walk through the drawbridge. "Thanks."

He shrugged and sat back down, looking out the window, and took a deep drag of his cigarette.

"Do you think it's okay if I leave my bag up here for the night?"

"I couldn't care less. Do what you want."

I took out the sleeping bag and tossed my hockey equipment in the corner. I'd started down the ladder when I heard Creeper ask, "Did you win?"

I popped my head back up. "We did. 4–2. First win of the season."

He made an ugly face. "Sounds like your team is garbage."

I climbed down, all the time thinking of my new sleeping bag. I bet Will and the others would be over-the-top jealous. As soon as I got to our store I unrolled it and slid in. It was soft and so warm it was like being in a furnace. After a minute I had to take my coat off and my shoes, and finally my pants. I felt bad about stealing it, especially after how nice Rasheed and Alisha and Rick had been.

I promised myself — no more stealing.

The last thing I remember before falling asleep was Alisha's green eyes.

Chapter 19

I peeked into Lewis's store. He'd been real scarce lately, which was actually a good thing because I hadn't had to tell him about W5. So I was kind of surprised to see him stretched out on the couch listening to his iPod. I had to wait like a minute before he noticed me.

"Don't be so shy, Mouse. You know you can come in any time. Have a seat and have some bread and peanut butter."

I knew he'd kill me if I came in without his permission, but I didn't say anything.

"Thanks. Maybe a little sandwich is good," I said. The truth was, I could have eaten the entire loaf.

"I hear some interesting things about you." He looked at me and laughed. "Apparently, we have a W5 problem."

I told Lewis what happened, and waited for him to freak on me. But he didn't — just the opposite.

With a wave of the hand, he told me to forget about W5. "I've got better things for you. You're too smart to deliver packages. It's a waste of your talents." He laughed again. "First, I got you something from the Goodwill, you know the one on Preston. They had this hanging outside the store. I think they call it a sidewalk sale."

He laughed real hard, as if it was the funniest thing in the world. "It was a good deal, all right. Those losers didn't even see me take it."

He pulled out a green coat and tossed it on my lap. "Try it on," he told me.

It was beyond ugly, but Lewis made such a thing about it, telling me how sick I looked and tough, that I didn't say anything bad. The hood even had gross fake fur around the edges, and it was Velcroed on — very weird. But the strangest thing was these huge pockets on the inside.

"Fits nice," he said. "I knew it. Perfect. I totally dig it, dude."

"Thanks, Lewis. I . . . uh . . . it's great."

I looked like a complete doofus.

"Why don't we hang out today," he said all sudden-like. "You doing anything?"

"Not really. Just going to the Market with J.J., and maybe Will and Rose. Dunno."

"Blow them off. Stick with me. I got a way to make way more money than hawking with them." He put an arm around my shoulders. "You're better than them, Mouse. You need to take advantage of your skills. Why waste your time hawking a few quarters a day just to give them to Rigger."

He said Rigger like it was a dirty word. No one

talked about Rigger like that. Of course, Lewis wasn't afraid of anyone.

He pointed toward my store. "I also noticed you picked up a sweet sleeping bag. Where'd you snatch that?"

It had been three weeks since I'd stolen it from Rasheed's van, but as much as I loved it, I couldn't shake the guilty feeling, and I didn't want to sound like a slimer to Lewis, so I lied.

"The army surplus store had it outside. I guess like what you called a sidewalk sale. I grabbed it when they weren't looking."

Lewis slapped the couch. "That's what I mean, Mouse. You're good, dude. That sleeping bag will keep you healthy. Keep your eyes open for stuff; stake a place out and make your move. You're small, so people won't notice you."

"Okay, Lewis."

He reached into another box and pulled out some bread and a jar of peanut butter, and handed me a Swiss Army knife from his pocket. It was a sweet knife, gleaming black with like a hundred blades and gadgets attached. I didn't waste any time making a sandwich. I had only eaten three Chinese buns yesterday, and I was starved.

"I hear you're still playing hockey?" he said.

I had to swallow hard to get the bread down. "I made a AA team. We won five games and then lost to the first-place team. We got a game tonight, and then three more after that. If we win two or three games we should make the playoffs, which is a miracle since we hadn't won a game before I joined." That last part sounded like bragging, and I wished I hadn't said it.

"I don't really like the idea of you hanging around Reggies . . . but I gotta admit I'm impressed. And it gives you something to do other than hawkin' with J.J." A look of disgust came over him when he mentioned J.J.

"You're right. He's so lame."

"Have one more piece and I want to go to the mall." He grabbed his knapsack.

I slathered another slice of bread with peanut butter and followed him to the ladder. This was going to be an awesome day. Hang with Lewis, and then a game tonight.

Chapter 20

I hadn't been to the mall since that lady had caught us in the stairwell. Lewis didn't seem too interested in the story when I tried to tell him on the way over. We went in and wandered around. Didn't seem like Lewis was interested in anything, least of all me, because he barely said a word the whole time. I knew better than to bug him with questions.

We'd walked to the end of the mall and back twice, when he steered me toward the food court. "You want some fries?" he asked.

I said, "Sure," even though that was maybe the dumbest question I'd ever heard. He even got me a large, which was cool because they were hot and perfectly crispy.

"You want any?" I offered.

Lewis shook his head.

"Big mistake. These are truly good fries. Are you sure?"

That pushed it. "I don't want your fries. Eat them yourself," he said in his tough voice. But then he laughed, and reached over and grabbed a few. "Thanks, Mouse. Maybe I will." He sat back and put his hands behind his head. "Hawking is kinda tough, ain't it?"

I munched down a few more fries and nodded.

"I used to be like you. Struggling to hawk some cash, lucky to get two bucks a day, and after you eat and pay Rigger or someone else for rent what do you got? A big fat zero, that's what."

I dug my fingers deep into the carton to get the last few fries.

"Hawking is a waste of time. So I'm gonna teach you how to make some real money — not two bucks a day, but two hundred."

"How can I do that?" It sounded impossible. Did Lewis make two hundred bucks a day?

"Are you finished?" he said, pointing to the carton.

"I am."

"Good. Come on and I'll show you." He pulled a hat out of his pocket and put it on, and then I followed him into an electronics store.

A skinny guy with a bright-red shirt was talking with a customer as we walked in, and another guy with the same red shirt stood behind the cash. Lewis led me to the other side of the store around a tall display unit. Before I could ask what we were doing here, Lewis stuffed some boxes into the pockets of my coat. It happened so fast I couldn't do anything. He just did it.

"Follow me," he ordered.

He stopped behind another display and stuffed more boxes into the inside coat pockets, and added these keychain-looking things into the outer pockets.

"What are you . . . ?"

"Shut up," he hissed. "Do what I tell you and everything will be fine. I'm going to buy something at the cash. Did you see the two white columns at the front of the store when we walked in?"

I nodded.

"Those are the alarms. You can't walk between them or the alarm will go off. But to the right there's a space, between the pillar and the window. I'm too big, but a little guy like you can sneak through no problem. Walk through that space and head out of the mall and wait for me."

He walked away before I could answer. The taste of the fries in my mouth made me feel sick and I suddenly felt like I had to go to the toilet real bad.

Lewis was talking to the guy at the cash. The skinny one was still dealing with the customer. If I tried to return the stuff to the shelves they'd see me for sure, not to mention Lewis would definitely kill me. What choice did I have? I tried to ignore the gross feeling in my gut and walked slowly to the front, pretending to look at some batteries.

I looked at the right column. Like Lewis said, there was a small space. I looked over to the cash. Lewis was handing the money over. He shot me a glance, which I knew meant get going!

I held my breath and walked out.

Nothing — no alarm. I'd made it.

"Can you come back to the store, please."

I felt a hand grab at my coat. I looked over my shoulder. It was the skinny guy, and he was laughing.

"I might want to see what's in those pockets," he said.

Not a good idea, I thought, so instead I started to run forward. He pulled hard on my hood. "No you don't," he said, still laughing.

I heard the crackling sound of Velcro separating. He stopped laughing pretty quick when the hood came off. I was free.

I ran like crazy, weaving in and out of people.

"Stop that kid!" he yelled.

A few Reggies looked at me funny but no one did anything. Up ahead I noticed the washroom sign, and that gave me an idea. I cut left and ran down the corridor and smashed into the door marked *No Exit*. I knew it led to the secret stairwell. I practically flew down the stairs and was sprinting down the street before I knew it.

I ran and ran and ran until I couldn't take another step. I just had to stop for a second. Hands on my knees, struggling to breathe. I looked around for any signs of the skinny guy, or anyone in a red shirt — or a security guard. I didn't see anyone and took off again, this time a bit slower. Only then did I notice I'd run all the way back to the train station. I figured I should keep going to the Underground and Lewis would meet me there. I wondered if he'd got caught.

Lewis was going to blame me for sure. But it wasn't my fault the skinny guy saw me. It was a lame plan. I had a coat that was like five times too big. And how obvious is it to try to sneak around the alarm columns? And why didn't he tell me what we were doing? I'd rather hawk all day than go through that again. No way was I stealing from a store again. I felt bad enough about the skates, and then the sleeping bag. But the skates were supposed to be a one-time thing. Without hockey my life would be . . . I don't know . . . not worth the trouble. And the sleeping bag, well, that was different because I needed it to stay warm. But this?

I pulled out something from the inside pockets. It was an iPod. The keychain things were memory sticks for computers. This stuff was expensive.

The drawbridge flew open and Rigger came out. I'd never seen him outside, and he didn't look too happy to see me.

"I told you guys no loitering," he barked.

"I'm not . . . loitering." I didn't know what the word meant, only that Rigger didn't like it. I knew Rigger would ask more questions, so I lied. "I'm waiting for Lewis. He told me to meet him here."

"I don't care. Beat it. You'll attract the cops, so get lost."

You didn't argue with Rigger, unless you wanted some bruises. I went back up the hill and was thinking of what to do next when I spotted Lewis waving at me across the street. A huge smile crossed his face as he came over.

"Mouse, that was grace under pressure. How'd you get away?"

I told him about the door to the stairway.

"That's using your street smarts, Mouse. I knew hawking was a waste of your talents." He pulled me toward the hill. "I wanna check out the haul."

"Rigger's down there," I said, pulling away. For some reason, I didn't like him touching me.

"Okay, fine. We'll go to the field behind the station."

Lewis talked the whole way about what a great team we were and how much money we were going to make together and another store he knew that would be twice as easy to steal from, and that now he could pay W5 the money he owed and he could do business with him again. He talked so fast my head was spinning. The whole time I couldn't stop thinking about what my mom would say. I'd once stolen a pack of gum from a store when I was a little kid and she'd made me take it right back and apologize. She was dead set against stealing. She used to call me her "angel boy." Those were the last words she ever said to me.

I wasn't an angel; I was a criminal.

When we got to the field, Lewis pulled all the stuff from my pockets. "Total score," he announced. "Two iPods, at least fifteen memory sticks, four iPod shuffles, and a few earphones to boot. Your first major heist, and it's a beauty." He stuffed it all into his knapsack. "I'm gonna move this stuff — and you'll get your share. Trust me. This is fantastic, and it's only the beginning. You did great. Tomorrow I have an even better idea."

"I don't want to do this again."

Lewis's head jerked back, like he'd been punched.

"*What?* You don't want to make lots of money?"

"I don't want to steal like that again. My mom told me . . ."

"What's your mom got to do with anything? We just made a ton of cash, and you're backing out on me, after everything I've done for you? Don't forget, I got you into the Underground." He looked at me real hard.

"I know, Lewis, and I'd do anything to help you, I swear. Only, I don't want to do this again. It's . . . It's . . ." I was going to say it's not right, but that would make him mad. "I just don't want to."

He shoved me in the chest and swung the knapsack onto his back. "You think you're a big shot? We'll see. You're called Mouse for a reason. I'll take this as pay-back for all the free stuff I gave you. Don't expect any more from me. Better yet, you should stay as far away from me as you can, if you know what's good for you. You can go hang with your hockey team, instead. Tell them you're a street kid, while you're at it. I bet they'd love to know that."

I watched Lewis stomp off. He was my best friend, I told myself. It would be okay. He had a bit of a temper. I just needed to let him calm down. Anyway, I guess I knew now how Lewis made so much money. He was a criminal. That's why he was into Fitzy's plan. And now I could also guess what was in the packages I delivered to W5.

Maybe I was no angel boy. But I hoped my mom would be proud of me right now, just a little.

Chapter 21

I took a deep breath. My legs were a bit shaky. I'd played practically the whole third period. We had to at least tie this game or we'd miss the playoffs. Things hadn't gone as well lately, and we'd lost two of our last four. And now it was down to this game. Everyone thought it would be no problem because it was against the Nationals, and they sucked. But here we were, down a goal, with just over a minute to go.

"Draw it back to me," Peter said, which is what he says every faceoff. That would be a great idea — so he could give the puck away! Sometimes I did it anyway because a few guys were giving me the gears about hogging the puck and too much ice time. Even the parents were making comments.

Rasheed tapped my shin pads. "We've got to get it in deep, so we can pull our goalie. Their winger will be parked at the top of the circle. Knock it to me and I'll get it out."

That sounded like a better plan.

"Let's get that goal, Rangers," Collin bellowed.

I'd been shadowed the entire game by this one guy, and sure enough there he was — a total pest, and dirty too. He'd been hooking and slashing me all game, and the ref hadn't called anything. He pointed to his winger, as if he were going to win the draw. Fat chance.

I watched the puck in the ref's hand, and slapped it to Rasheed. Unfortunately, their left winger got on it quick, and Rasheed couldn't get enough on it to send it out of our zone. Their defenceman wired it back along the wall and around the net, with Peter in pursuit and Collin in front.

I checked out the time — one minute. Great! The game would be over before we touched the puck. I drifted into the slot.

"Get outta my way, runt," the centre said, and he cross-checked me in the back. As usual, the refs did nothing.

"Don't feel like it," I said, and slashed his ankle real quick. Before I had a chance to enjoy his reaction, the jerk gave me a butt-end into my side. It hurt bad. I was happy that Collin came over. "I got him covered," he said, which let me go after the puck. I was glad to be rid of him.

Rasheed and Peter were battling two Nationals for the puck. Rasheed spotted me when I was about ten feet away. He grabbed a guy's stick and was able to kick the puck free. I figured he'd get a penalty for that, and maybe the Nationals did too because they slowed down.

But the refs didn't call it, and lucky for me because I finally had the puck without that centre all over me. I spun around in the corner and headed up ice. Derrick cut across the blue line. I held onto it. There was time for me to take one more rush. No point passing.

I got across centre and raced in on their defence. Like a doofus one of them tried to hit me at the blue line. I dangled him and bounced outside easy enough. It was a two-on-one with Derrick on my right, yelling for a pass. That bugged me. I do all the work and he wants the glory. So I faked it, and let a shot rip for the top corner on the goalie's glove hand. The goalie dropped into his butterfly and got his glove on it. Maybe I should have passed.

But the hockey gods were on my side. The goalie muffed it. The puck nicked the top of his glove and rolled in. The next second I was sliding into the boards face first. That moron centre drilled me after I scored.

Rasheed pulled me to my feet. "You're off the freakin' hook, dude. We kill this thirty seconds and we're into the playoffs."

I tapped his shin pads. "Goalie's a total loser. Can't believe he let that in."

Collin came over and gave me a tap on the helmet with his glove. "I knew you'd score. Never any doubt."

I took my time skating over to the bench to enjoy the moment. The guys were acting real calm about it. I figured they'd be more hyped, but it made sense when I thought about it because there was still time on the clock. So I stayed low-key too. Near the bench Derrick came over and said to me, "Why didn't you pass? I had an open net."

128

The guy was so lame. "I scored. What's your problem?"

"Forget it," he said.

That killed the fun a bit. I guess I probably should have passed. The goal was lucky and Derrick would have scored for sure. I admit I was getting a bit worried about what the other guys thought about me. I knew Rasheed and Collin were buds. The others were nice enough, although I once heard Derrick call me The Hog. Maybe I deserved it. Malcolm was constantly giving me a hard time about passing.

A few parents were yelling from the stands.

"Keep it out of our end, Rangers."

"Play it safe."

The whistle blew. "Nationals timeout," the ref said.

I reached over the boards and grabbed a water bottle, and we crowded around our coaches. "This is where we want to be," Lou said. "They're going to pull their goalie, so let's keep the puck in their end. And no icing. We don't want faceoffs in our zone. Wingers play it absolutely safe. Off the boards and out. Defencemen, put it off the glass if you have to. No soft clearances at our blue line." He pointed at me. "Jacob, take over for Jonny at centre. Change it up."

I was in shock. I'd just scored the goal to put us in the playoffs and he was taking me off for Jacob. I pushed the door so hard it made a big crash, and sat down, leaning against the wall.

Malcolm leaned over me. "I've been talking to you about passing. Derrick was wide open there. I'm glad you scored, but you got lucky. The smart play was the pass. The defenceman and the goalie were playing you all the way."

I knew he was right, but I was so angry about getting taken off . . . well . . . I lost it a bit. "If I score ten goals you still diss me. That's all you ever do, and it's getting real lame."

A hard look came into his eyes. "That's not how we talk to a coach on this team. I'm trying . . ." He took a breath. "I'm trying to teach you about hockey, about teamwork."

A huge roar interrupted him. He and I looked up at the same time. Peter was chasing a guy who had a clear breakaway. I couldn't believe it.

Real close to the net the guy made a move to his backhand and Andrew slid across in a butterfly; only too much, and when the guy switched the puck to his forehand, he had an easy shot to the glove side.

So the moron rings it right off the post. I swear. He missed it. I started laughing like a maniac it was that bizarre. Peter slapped the rebound to the corner and Rasheed did the rest, skating the puck to centre and dumping it in. The buzzer rang to end the game before the Nationals could even get the puck out of their zone.

The Rangers had made the playoffs.

Chapter 22

All the guys jumped the boards and charged Andrew in net. I gave Malcolm a look when I left, as if to say, that's what happens when you take me off.

"Great game," I said to Derrick. I figured I should try to make it up to him for not passing.

He obviously didn't hear because he went over and began pounding Rasheed and Collin on the helmets.

"Way to hold the fort, Andrew," I said to our goalie.

He mumbled, "Thanks," and skated over to Jacob and Peter.

"On to the playoffs," I said to Rasheed. Derrick shrugged and joined Jacob and Peter.

"You were on fire again," Collin said, kind of mellow this time.

"What happened at the end? Did Peter give the puck away?" I said. I still could not believe Lou had taken me off. Rasheed looked away and Collin tapped his stick on the ice a few times.

"I didn't see what happened. Malcolm was ragging on me at the bench," I said.

"I guess we didn't need that last breakaway. But we're in the playoffs," Rasheed said.

"Let's line up, Rangers," Peter said.

I joined the end of the line and began shaking hands with the Nationals. About halfway I noticed I was getting close to that centre who'd shadowed me. I braced myself for anything, even a punch.

"Great game," he said to me. "Good luck in the playoffs."

He moved on before I could say anything. That was weird. I thought he hated me. This entire game was weird, and it continued in the dressing room. I figured everyone would be going nuts, but it was real quiet, and the guys were just getting undressed. Lou usually came in right away and spoke to us, but not this time.

I was an expert at listening to people talk without them knowing I could hear. That's how I heard the gossip lining up for the washroom in the morning, or figured out was going on in Executive Alley. So when I saw Peter, Derrick, and Andrew speaking quietly to each other I decided to listen in. I opened my bag and bent forward pretending to be looking for something.

"Stink Bomb's such a puck hog. I know he can put the puck in the net, but he could pass once in a while," Peter said.

Is that what they called me? Puck Hog was one thing — but Stink Bomb? Did I smell that bad? Really?

"Try playing on his line," Derrick said. "He couldn't care less about this team. Malcolm talks to him every game and he still never passes."

"The team was more fun when we were losing," Andrew said.

"So what if he can score. I'd score too if I never passed," Derrick said next.

I began to untie my skates, all the while listening intently.

"My dad's talking to Lou right now," Derrick continued. "He's so mad, he wants him off the team."

"And he didn't even pay. That's what my dad says," Peter added.

"Ever seen a guy wear the same clothes every day of his life? No wonder he smells," Andrew started laughing.

"Try sitting next to him on the bench," Derrick said.

"No thanks," Andrew said, laughing harder.

"Collin told me Rasheed plugs his nose when he gets into their van," Peter said. All three were laughing now.

Rasheed actually did that? What did Alisha think of me?

"He lives in a nice house, I think. Rasheed's seen it. But it's weird. Is he poor or something? If his family doesn't have the money, okay. But I don't think it's right that he gets a free ride just because he can score," Peter said.

"And the guy has Graf skates. I mean — come on," Andrew said.

"I know Rasheed's dad is tired of having to drive him all the time," Derrick said.

"Rasheed and his dad are too nice to say anything," Andrew said.

"It was his idea to get Stink Bomb on the team. He should be the one to suffer," Derrick said, and they laughed.

I stopped listening, and I ripped my equipment off. So they called me Stink Bomb, did they! Bunch of stupid Reggies, I thought. Idiots. I'm done with the Rangers. I'm taking my skates, gloves and stick, and I'm out of here. I tied the skate laces together and threw the skates over my shoulder. One of the skates banged into my ribs and it hurt, but I was way too mad to care.

I went over to the door to grab my stick. Someone's stick was crossed over mine, so I pulled on it real hard and all the sticks fell to the ground. A few bounced off a garbage can and made a huge racket, like someone drumming.

"Smooth, Einstein," Derrick wisecracked.

I kicked the sticks to the side and one hit Andrew on the leg.

"Watch it. What are you doing?" he said, his face all screwed up tight.

"You're all such a bunch of losers, I can't believe it!" I screamed at him.

His face turned beet red.

"You think you're so smart? I know everything. Only reason I stuck around was I felt sorry for you losing every game. You want me off the team — fine. This team is a joke — a total joke — and I don't need to waste my time."

I pointed at Rasheed. "You don't have to plug your nose anymore." Then I pointed at Derrick. "You want me to pass the puck? Well, it's your puck now. You score since you're so great."

I spit on Derrick's bag, I was so insanely mad, and flung the door open and left. Lou and Malcolm were talking to some parents off to the side, including Rick and Derrick's father.

"Hey there, Jonny," Lou said, all friendly. "That was some effort tonight. Can I just have a quick word with you before you go to talk about . . ."

Like I was going to have a nice chat. "I left your smelly equipment in the smelly dressing room, so get off my back."

Lou's eyebrows got all tight together. "Why are you yelling at me? I only want to discuss . . ."

"I know what you wanna say. You think I smell. Well, you're fat and stupid and ugly . . . and stupid. I'm done with this team and I can't believe I bothered playing."

"Jonathon, you need to calm down," Rick said.

"You need to shut up!" I yelled back. "I know you're all mad that I didn't pay. But I ain't gonna. Here's two bucks, and get Rasheed's skates sharpened 'cause he can't skate for nothing." I threw the money at Rick and hit him right in the chest. I watched the coin spin around and around on the ground until it toppled and stopped.

Only then did I notice everyone staring at me, all the Rangers' parents and strangers too. Rasheed and

Collin stood in front of the dressing room door, in their hockey pants and shin pads, their mouths wide open. I knew I had to leave or I'd start to bawl, and I wasn't going to give them the satisfaction.

Soon I was outside, running through the parking lot toward the street. I remembered turning right when we got here, so I went left to get to the main street. That's when I heard my name called over and over. It was Alisha. I stopped and turned around. She was the one person who always treated me well. At least I could say goodbye to her.

"Jonathon, where are you going? How are you getting home?"

"I called my uncle," I lied. "He's coming to get me."

Rick came up behind her. "We don't deserve this type of treatment," he said. I could see he was steaming mad. "I've given you a lift to every game and practice."

"You're like the rest," I sneered back. "You can't fool me. I saw you talking with Derrick's dad. You all want me off the team." I stomped my foot. "You don't like my smell . . . well . . . I don't like you, or Rasheed, or the Rangers . . . or Alisha."

"I hate you all — stupid Reggies!"

Rick looked all serious at me. "I'll wait until your uncle arrives. But I don't understand where you got this idea anyone wanted you off the team. No one does. I can tell you that."

It didn't matter. There was no going back anyway. And besides, Reggies always lie. You can't trust them.

Lewis told me that, and I'd seen it with my own eyes a million times. They promise you some money and then never give it, or they snatch you from the streets and put you in juvie. "I don't need your help. My uncle will meet me at the corner. I called him on my cell phone."

I wanted to say more only the words wouldn't come out, so I turned and left. Playing hockey with a bunch of Reggies was plain dumb of me. So hockey was done. Fine! Big deal.

Stink Bomb!

Stupid Reggies!

Chapter 23

The sun was down and it was getting real cold. I hopped off the sidewalk to go down the hill to the Underground. My head was still dizzy and I couldn't think straight, and I'd had to buy a subway ticket, which was money I really did not want to spend. All the way back on the subway I'd gone over the game, and what I heard in the dressing room, and what Rick said to me. I remembered a bunch of times when I maybe could have passed to open guys. Most of the time I thought I could do it better myself, and I did score two goals. I guess I was a bit of a hog, and I probably did stink, and my clothes were dirty.

I did the secret knock and waited. Nothing happened, so I did it again, and the door opened a crack. Brachy peeked out.

"Mouse has arrived," he said, with a laugh. "Rigger wants a conversation right now." He pulled the door open a little more and I slid in.

"What's he want?" All I wanted to do was curl up in my sleeping bag.

"Go ask," Brachy said with a smirk, and he sat back on the chair.

It would be a waste of time asking him for info, so I headed down the ladder. I should have put my skates, gloves and stick in my hiding place. It was totally awkward trying to carry them down. The stupid skates banged into my sides, and climbing down a ladder with hockey gloves is no picnic, either.

Rigger was spread out on his chair, one leg sprawled over an armrest, sipping on a drink that smelled like coffee.

He held out his palm. "Any chance I'm gonna get paid, Mouse?" he said.

I pulled out fifty cents and put it in his hand. He shook his head.

"This ain't no charitable institution. You owe me five bucks."

"I do not! I only owe for tonight."

"What about the hockey equipment you stored and didn't tell me about?" He swung his feet to the floor. "Nobody rips me off. I'm charging you extra for that. So it's five bucks or you're outta here." He put his leg back on the armrest.

I felt my own legs tremble. I didn't have five bucks, and like a jerk I'd thrown two bucks away after the game.

"I'll borrow it. Can I go ask? Please. Give me a second."

He laughed real low. "Sure, little Mouse. Take your time."

I hated Rigger so much, and that stupid chair so

much, and this stupid Underground. This was the day of jerks.

I hurried to my store. I'd never been so glad to see Will and Rose. Will was leaning against the wall, and Rose was lying on the floor. I forced myself to sound like nothing was wrong. "Hey guys, how's it going?"

Rose squinted up at me. Will folded his arms; and neither answered my question. That unnerved me a bit. I coughed a few times to cover up and decided to just hit them up for the cash.

"I'm a little short today for Rigger. You know what he's like. I left my hockey bag here one night and now he wants five bucks. Can I borrow it and I'll pay you back tomorrow for sure?"

All I got was more silence.

"I ain't playing hockey no more so I got lots of time to hawk the money, and it's getting warmer so . . . no problem." I couldn't stop my voice from quivering. "Do you have the money?"

Rose turned her back to me.

"Why don't you ask your buddy Lewis?" Will said. He seemed to be laughing at me. Did he know about Lewis and me having that fight?

"I could, sure. I just figured since we were . . ."

"We were what, Mouse?" Will said, real harsh.

"Since we were friends, and lived in this store together . . . and I've bought you stuff . . . and . . ."

"I am not inclined to provide you with credit at the moment," Will said. "Perhaps you could make a withdrawal from your bank account — or I encourage you to ask your friend Lewis — or J.J. for that matter."

Rose laughed. A sinking feeling trickled down my chest into my stomach. Undergrounders always lent money for rent. But then Will was a jerk.

"Whatever," I snapped. "Don't ask me for help the next time you need cash."

Rose's laughing totally unnerved me. Everyone seemed to be in on some joke except me, and just when I needed them to be serious. Lewis was my last hope. We were buddies, even if we had a bit of a fight. He always looked out for me, and this was nothing for him. Besides, he really did owe me something for the stuff I stole.

As I headed back to Executive Alley, Creeper was coming the other way. Now here's a guy who'd owed me money for like two months.

"Hey, Creeper. How's it going?"

He grimaced. "It's . . . going like any other freakin' day."

He tried to walk past me and I grabbed his arm.

"Can I get that three dollars I lent you? Remember? I lent you two bucks, and then another one. That's three bucks."

"I gave you a subway ticket."

"Okay. Then you owe me $2.25."

"No."

That word hurt like a slap in the face. "You owe me the money. Come on. I need it. Rigger's being totally lame and I gotta pay him or he said I can't stay tonight."

Creeper shrugged. "Then go," he said, and tried to walk away again.

I grabbed his arm, and he shoved me hard in the chest and pulled his arm free. "Touch me again, and I'll break you in half."

"What's wrong with everyone?" That shaky sound was in my voice, and I couldn't stop this panicky feeling from bugging my stomach.

Creeper raised his eyes to the ceiling and then leaned forward and whispered, "You're jacked, Mouse. Rigger said. You should just get your stuff and go." And with that he went into his store.

My legs were numb, I couldn't move, and I had a bizarre feeling that I had to go pee. The panic in my gut had taken over my whole body. Jacked meant Rigger kicked you out for good. In my time, only one kid had been jacked, and he'd been caught stealing from Executive Alley. I hadn't done anything.

I needed Lewis.

As luck would have it he was standing outside his store eating a sandwich. I ran up to him.

"Lewis . . . Lewis . . ." I stammered. "Creeper told me Rigger wants to jack me. Do you know what's going on? I mean, I didn't do nothing. Why is he asking for five bucks when I don't owe him a penny? I only left my bag up top for one night, and he's gone crazy about it. I'll pay, but I need a loan or he's going to jack me."

I think I was crying, but I was so messed I wasn't sure. Lewis took no notice of me and chewed his sandwich. I waited for him to speak, which was painful because now I had to go pee real bad. Finally, he swallowed his food.

"So Mouse wants Lewis to help him? Is that it?"

All I could muster was a nod.

"And when Lewis asked Mouse for help, what did Mouse say?"

"I'll help you anytime," I said weakly.

He poked me in the chest. "Did you help me, Mouse, or not?"

"I was a jerk. I admit it, totally. I was tired from running, and scared. I trust you. I'll help you with whatever. We can . . . do you need a package delivered? Or we can go to the electronics store?"

"You've been replaced, Mouse, but thanks for the generous offer." That's when I noticed J.J. stretched out on Lewis's couch, grinning at me all smug-like, and laughing like all the others.

It was over. Lewis had actually sold me out, all because I wouldn't steal for him.

I marched slowly to Rigger.

"Have we managed to borrow the money?" he mocked.

I shook my head.

"Then it's time for you to leave."

"Can I come back tomorrow with the money?" It didn't sound like my voice.

Rigger yawned. "You're not dependable. I think it's time for you to find a new place to sleep."

There it was — officially jacked.

"Why?" I had to know.

He looked surprised. "Lewis got you in — and Lewis got you out."

Suddenly, I couldn't stand being here; the sight of Rigger made me beyond angry. If only I could grow big and smash his face to pieces and then I'd sit in his throne chair and tell people what to do. But I was twelve years old, and the growing would have to wait.

I went back to my store to get my stuff.

"Here Mousey, Mousey, Mousey," Fitzy called out in a high voice, and Happy D began giggling like an idiot as usual. Then, as if things couldn't get worse, Will was lying in my sleeping bag and he had this stupid goofy grin like he just won a million dollars in the lottery.

"I'm leaving," I said to Will and Rose. "I know you think it's funny, but Rigger's jacked me, or I think Lewis did it. So laugh away — and real funny with the sleeping bag." Will rolled over as if he was going to sleep. "Real funny. Now give it over." He didn't move. I grabbed the end of the bag and began to pull on it. Will sat up violently and took hold of my wrist, and for all my struggling I couldn't pull away.

"Give the poor kid his freakin' sleeping bag." Rose was on her knees glaring at her brother.

He let go of me, but not my sleeping bag.

"Stop torturing him. Why are you so ugly and mean?" she yelled.

Will spun toward her. "*Why?* Because we're living like freakin' animals, underground, hawking on the streets, freezing cold all the time! Because I gotta sneak around so W5 don't kill me, and we gotta kiss that jerk Rigger's butt, so he lets us in every night. Because I wouldn't mind sleeping in a real bed once in a while and eating as much as I want, and I didn't ask to have a dad who got drunk all the time . . ."

Rose was crying but not making a sound.

"Why am I so mean?" Will hissed. "It's called staying alive, and I don't see why I have to sleep in some thin, pathetic, dirty little sleeping bag."

"He's a little kid," Rose answered. "He'll die out there without his sleeping bag. You want to kill him?"

"I couldn't care less," Will spat back. But then he climbed out and threw the sleeping bag in my face. "There — happy?" he growled at Rose, and he took his sleeping bag from the corner and began to spread it out.

Rose and my eyes met. She looked like nothing had happened, and without a word lay back down.

A minute later I was climbing up the ladder with my skates slung over my shoulder, stick in hand, and the rest of my stuff in my knapsack. I don't even know why I was taking my hockey stuff. I just couldn't stand to leave anything here.

I clambered over the top and looked down. I hated this place. Will was right. We lived like animals.

But at least it was a home. Now I was a Streeter.

Chapter 24

I stared in the window for a minute. The red neon S in the Baxter's sign flickered on and off. So much had happened since I'd stolen the skates. It was hard to believe I'd been better off then. I yawned for like the millionth time today. I hadn't slept too well last night; I was too nervous someone was going to steal my stuff, and a doorway isn't a comfortable place to sleep.

The most important thing was to eat. I hadn't had a thing since yesterday before the game. Funny how important the game had been, and now I couldn't care less — I had way bigger problems than playing hockey with a bunch of idiots. I needed to hawk some money real bad. I kept walking for a while and then stopped by the hill at Cedarview Park to watch some guys skating around on the outdoor rink.

Just then something thumped me in the stomach and all my wind left me and I could hardly breathe. I dropped to my knees, and a boot stepped hard on my fingers. I tried to pull my hand away.

"Let go. Let go," I begged.

He did — and I wished he hadn't.

Because staring down at me was W5.

"This morning I met Lewis's new delivery boy. I guess we don't get to see you no more." He leaned over and slapped me in the face, and I could taste blood in my mouth. "And I guess you ain't got Lewis to protect you no more either — not that I care about him. That dude is almost as lame as you."

He laughed real ugly and then he kicked me in the ribs. The pain went up my side into my skull and then all the way back down to my feet. I couldn't think straight.

"And the new kid isn't so dumb as to mess with me — and he doesn't think he's a tough guy."

He pulled me to my knees by my hair and punched me in the eye. It hurt too much to cry.

"You think you can mess with me and get away with it? Do you?"

"I'm sorry. I'm sorry. I'm sorry."

W5 began to mimic me and his crew all laughed. "Let's see how this rock rolls," he said, and the next thing I knew I was tumbling down a steep hill, bouncing off the hard, crusty snow and ice. My cheek stung as I got up — I must have scraped it on the way down — and my head was all wobbly.

"Have fun with him, boys. I gotta split," W5 said, loud enough for me to hear, and he walked off.

Scrunchy Face and three of his friends looked down at me from the top of the hill.

"We'll give you a ten-second head start before we

come down and beat some respect into you," Scrunchy Face yelled.

"Why the head start?" one friend said loudly.

Scrunchy Face made a big deal of shrugging his shoulders. "So let's do it."

They came running after me. All I really wanted to do was curl up and cry — definitely not a good plan. Instead, I ran across the field, but they were behind me in no time, the sound of their feet on the snow getting louder and louder.

"Look at the little guy go."

"He's so cute."

"Nowhere to hide this time."

They were right. No garbage bin to jump into. I figured the change room, which was uphill and over to my right, was my only hope. Maybe someone would be there. I turned that way and began scampering up the hill, praying I wouldn't slip and fall.

About halfway up I lost my footing on a patch of ice, and flopped to my knees. It hurt like anything, but I was too terrified to care. I began crawling up the hill, which actually worked better than walking, although Scrunchy Face and his buds thought it was hilarious.

"He's so scared he's crawling like a baby."

"You need a diaper change?"

They could laugh away, and my knees were burning, but crawling got me to the top way before them, and I sprinted my guts out across the parking lot and into the change room.

Empty!

I froze — rooted to the floor like an ice statue — in the middle of the room, trapped, with nowhere to run, no one to help me. I had that pee feeling again.

Scrunchy Face opened the door, hands on his knees, breathing heavy. "That run is gonna cost you ten head shots." He turned to his friends. "I'm tired of chasing this shrimp. Let's break his legs so he stays in one place."

They all laughed like a bunch of monkeys.

"You leave now — or I call police."

The janitor held his mop like a sword and he pointed it at them. Scrunchy Face took a step forward — and so did the janitor.

Something about that janitor convinced Scrunchy Face to back down. Something about him was tough. Scrunchy Face thumbed toward the door and said, "Maybe we'll continue this party later. Talk to you soon, Mouse." He nodded at me a few times, and off they went. I watched them skid down the hill and back across the field.

"I not see you for long time," the janitor said.

"I . . . I guess . . . Well, I was playing hockey with a team and . . . I guess I didn't have time to play here much . . . anymore."

"You good player. I play hockey very much in Soviet Union when I am young man."

"Thanks. And thanks for saving me from those guys. They . . . well . . . they don't like me too much."

He sat on a bench and leaned his head toward me. "You are okay? You are hurt?"

"I'm okay. Banged my knees a bit is all. Those guys are too slow to catch me, anyway."

He looked at me. "It look like they catch you little bit."

It was funny how he said it, and it made me laugh. "Maybe a little. But I'm okay now. Thanks again." I looked outside and couldn't see Scrunchy Face or his friends anymore. "I gotta go. I'll see ya."

He nodded and went back to his mop and pail, and I went out the door. I waved from the outside and he waved back. The clang of the closing door bugged me a bit. I was back on the streets.

I ran as fast as I could, away from Scrunchy Face and his friends, ignoring the pain in my knees. I ran until my lungs were about to explode, until I could barely breathe, until I was almost sick, until I was so tired I forgot what had happened to me.

But I didn't stop. Because I knew when I stopped running, I would remember everything.

Chapter 25

Later that afternoon I was hawking at a park in the west end. I didn't do so hot — only got $2.50. I probably didn't look too clean and scared people off. Lewis had always told me Reggies were afraid of Streeters that were real dirty.

It was getting a bit dark, and I still hadn't eaten. Around now usually W5 and his crew would be at the TV station, so I figured I could safely get a couple of Chinese buns for dinner. I had to get my sleeping bag at the Theatre anyway. As I walked, I cheered up when I remembered I didn't have to save money for rent and could get an extra bun; at least that was one good thing about getting jacked.

Even though it wasn't that cold, I was shivering from being outside all day. The wind had picked up, which didn't help. To make me more miserable my head wasn't feeling too good, and I was having trouble looking out of my eye where W5 punched me. My pants had bloodstains, and my knees hurt because my pants rubbed against them with each step.

I was too hungry to care about what I looked like anyway, and I put a dollar down on the counter.

"Two coconut buns, please."

Winston leaned over the counter. "What happened to eye?" he demanded.

Was it that bad?

"I fell. Can I have two buns, please?"

"You be careful. That bad bruise around eye. Very dangerous."

The smell of the shop was torture for my stomach. I pointed at the buns. Winston grunted and put four buns in a bag.

"Two extra for today — no charge."

He dropped the dollar into the cash register — and then he laughed. I looked at him with my mouth wide open. He actually laughed.

I'd won the bet, for whatever that's worth.

The moment was ruined when the door opened and Will, Rose and J.J. came in.

Rose's eyes bugged out. "You run into a truck, Mouse?"

This was their fault. If they'd given me the five bucks I'd still be safe in the Underground. If J.J. hadn't made me go to the TV station, W5 never would have pounded me in the first place. I wouldn't be a Streeter now.

"That's about the dumbest thing I've ever heard, like I actually ran into a truck. You're as dumb as a truck." Then I thought of a great diss. "So what happened to *your* face? Oh yeah. I forgot. You were born that way."

Rose looked like she'd been slapped in the face. "I'm just asking if you're hurt . . . is all."

"You watch your mouth," Will threatened. "You ain't got Lewis as backup no more."

I lost it. My fist thundered into his nose and he dropped to his knees, blood pouring onto the floor.

"Get out now!" Winston yelled. "Get out and don't come back."

I pushed J.J. aside, glared at Rose, and left. By the time I got to the Theatre, I'd already inhaled all four buns, either because I was so hungry or so angry. All my junk was safe, at least, and I calmed down. Hitting Will sure felt good at the time, but now my right hand began to throb. Was there a part of my body that didn't hurt?

I grabbed my sleeping bag. I didn't much fancy sleeping in a doorway again, and the wind still hadn't let up and it wasn't that warm. At the corner I crouched down and looked for any sign of W5 or Scrunchy Face or Will. Lewis had taught me that trick. People don't notice you down low.

Lewis! What did he know anyway — the stupid traitor? I was glad that I wouldn't have to hang with him anymore.

My knees were really bugging me, and it was hard to see out of my eye it was so swollen. I'd have killed to lie down and sleep, but it's not that easy to find a safe spot in the middle of a big city. There were people everywhere, and cars and noise. I crossed onto Macdonald Avenue and headed toward the lake. I'd heard about a park where Streeters went to sleep. I was nervous about it, though. No one knew me, and maybe it was dangerous, but it couldn't be worse than walking around all night.

Suddenly, I heard the roar of the subway under my feet and the ground shook a bit, warm wind blowing up in my face. Without realizing it, I had walked over the vents, the perfect sleeping spot. A few people walked by, but I didn't care. The drunks weren't around — it was probably too early for them. I could sleep for an hour here and then check the park out. I squeezed into my sleeping bag and pulled the top over my head.

○ ○ ○

The side of my face hit the ground first, but my knees slamming into the steel grate hurt the most. I screamed without understanding what was going on.

"It's a little kid," someone said, his words slurred.

"What's a little kid doin' here?" his friend asked.

"I'd like to teach this little kid to have some respect for his elders," he slurred again.

I blinked a few times. I could make out two men staring down at me. One was holding my sleeping bag. They'd lifted me right into the air and poured me out like a pile of garbage. I leapt to my feet.

The guy with my sleeping bag stepped toward me. Because he was so drunk, he wasn't that quick, so I got out of the way fairly easy. I reached for my sleeping bag and pulled on it. "Give me that; it's mine," I said.

"No it's not," he mumbled, and he pulled back.

The slurring guy charged toward me and knocked me down. I landed on my hip.

"This is our grate!" he shouted. "Go rot yourself, you . . ." He hiccuped and blinked at me a bunch of times. "Got rot yourself," he repeated.

I got back up. Neither one seemed too steady on his feet, so I made my move and tried to yank the sleeping bag back. I almost got it but the guy did a 360 spin and the sleeping bag wrapped around his body, and then he fell like a log to the ground. I pulled on it, but I may as well have tried to push over a giant tree.

The slurring guy growled, and he swung his foot at me. But the doofus missed completely, whirled around on one foot and fell on his friend, so now the two of them were lying on my sleeping bag.

"Get off me, you fat slob," the first guy moaned.

The slurring guy started laughing, which set the other guy off and soon they were laughing like hyenas, and then they seemed to forget I was there and fell asleep. They both just feel asleep, all bundled up with my freakin' sleeping bag. I laughed too, even though this was a total disaster — my sleeping bag kidnapped by two drunks. I tried pulling it free but it was useless.

All of a sudden it didn't seem so funny. Those drunks could fall asleep as if they didn't have any worries. I had plenty. I had so many worries I had that sick feeling in my stomach. That feeling was becoming my best friend because it never left me.

This was real bad. I had to get some sleep, somewhere safe, and out of this wind, or . . . well, I really wasn't sure if I'd make it. This was worse than when I first hit the streets after mom died and Ron took off on me, because now it was winter and now I really understood what it meant to be on the streets, alone, without a sleeping bag or anywhere to go.

You can't survive like that; you just can't.

Chapter 26

I was feeling dizzy and sick at the same time, maybe because I'd been walking around for hours. There was no point waiting for those moron drunks to let my sleeping bag go, so I finally went to check out that park. A few Streeters were huddled under an open building. All of them had sleeping bags. I couldn't see myself joining them, so I left.

My next plan was to find an open door and sneak into a garage. I couldn't think of anything better. I figured that once I got out of the wind it wouldn't be that cold, and I might get lucky and find a blanket or something. I went to the alley near the outdoor rink. There was a whole row of garages there and one of them had to be open.

I knew it was risky, but I didn't care. I'd worry about tomorrow . . . well, tomorrow.

I started pulling on the handles one by one — nothing. I even twisted one so hard I think I broke it. One after the other: locked, locked, locked. I got to the last garage — locked again! I dropped to my knees. I was so tired. It was like someone was trying to kill me.

Now what? I could try some more garages, but I didn't know of any other alleyways like this where I could get into a garage without having to sneak into someone's backyard. Think, Jonathon, think . . . but for some reason my brain wasn't turned on, or it was dead, or frozen. Now what? The question kept repeating itself, and I had no answer. This was nuts. Houses everywhere and all of them locked — to keep me out. How unfair was that? Why did Rigger run the Underground anyway? No one should own it. I should own it. Why not?

Rigger's an idiot, and so's Lewis,
and Will,
and Rose,
and J.J.,
and Creeper, Happy D, Fitzy, Skidder, W5,
    Scrunchy Face, and the drunks,
and Lou and Malcolm,
and Peter, Derrick, Andrew, Collin, Rasheed . . .

Rasheed! He lived around here, and he had a huge garage in his backyard. I'd seen it when I went to help Rasheed get his equipment, and best of all it wasn't even attached to the house. No one would know I was there. I could sneak in and be gone before anyone woke up.

I cheered up and I swear it felt like only a minute before I spotted his house up ahead. Funny how a great idea can give you energy. The lights in the house were all off — not surprising because it must have been pretty late, and also lucky because that meant they were all asleep. When I got close I ducked down behind a large hedge between Rasheed's place and his next-door neighbour's, and made my way along the driveway, all hunched over and pushing my back real tight against the hedge. A final check — nothing seemed to be doing in the house — and I got past the front steps and high-tailed it to the garage.

I twisted the garage handle, praying it wouldn't be locked. Bingo! It was open. It squeaked a bit but not too bad. I pulled it up only enough to slide underneath on my belly, and closed it back up. Once inside I turned the light on. There were no windows, but I was nervous all the same, and I quickly scanned the shelves for anything to sleep on.

To the right was the most beautiful thing I'd ever seen: camping equipment, all organized on shelves. They had coolers, tents, and chairs — and a bunch of sleeping bags. I pulled a grey and a red one down, and then spotted a few mats. I grabbed one of those and spread it out on the floor. Maybe my luck wasn't so bad after all. I hadn't had such a comfortable bed in ages. It was almost as good as Lewis's couch, and the sleeping bag was the same kind I'd stolen from Rasheed before.

Stupid drunks! I hope they choked on that sleeping bag.

The garage creaked with the howling wind. It felt so good not to be outside. My face felt weird now that the wind wasn't blowing on it all the time. I was so tired that I had become light-headed, and my legs and arms were tingly. As I closed my eyes, my mom's face popped into my head. It does that sometimes; I never know when. It could be in the morning, or just walking along, but usually it's when I'm falling asleep. This time she was smiling, and her hair was all done up like when she was getting fancy to go out to dinner. I wondered if she was looking down on me now.

I hope not. I think she'd have been sad to see me like this.

○ ○ ○

I was dreaming about being in a park or in a forest with big trees and there were voices, kids' voices, all around, and they were talking like kids do at a playground, and then there were storm clouds and huge thunder, and a big flash of light appeared, not exactly lightning, but as if God had suddenly turned on the sun and made the world light, although it was all foggy and I couldn't see too much. Then I heard a scream, which set my heart pounding through my chest. I sat up and looked around in a daze because the dream was so real and it took me a while to see that I wasn't really in a forest.

The fog cleared. Rasheed and Alisha were staring at me, and then I knew what had happened. The voices I'd heard were Rasheed and Alisha, the thunder was them opening the garage door, and the sunlight meant I'd slept in. It was morning. I was trapped, and wrapped up in a sleeping bag so I couldn't even make a run for it.

Alisha spoke first, and her voice really freaked me out because she sounded so scared and her voice cracked. "What happened to you, Jonathon? Are you hurt?"

160

That was a bizarre question. I'm sleeping in their garage and the first thing she asks is if I'm hurt?

Rasheed spoke next. "Why aren't you at home?"

I spotted the red sleeping bag, which was still in its nylon bag. I needed it. Without answering, I wiggled out of the grey sleeping bag and grabbed the red one, and got to my knees.

"Talk to us, Jonathon. What's going on?" Alisha pleaded.

I did something dumb and looked at her. She looked beyond shocked, as if she'd seen a Martian or something, and her eyes were watering, not crying but wet. I figured I had to say something. Besides, I still felt awful about how I'd yelled at her after I quit the team.

"Don't worry about me," I said, more calmly than I thought possible. "Pretend I wasn't here. I won't bug you anymore. Sorry. But I gotta take this or I'm gonna die," and I held up the red sleeping bag. "I'll bring it back when it gets warmer or I find another, I promise."

"1 gotta go — now," I said, in what I hoped was a tough-guy voice. "Don't try to stop me, I'm warning you. I mean it."

Rasheed held out his hand. "Calm down, Jonathon. Tell us what happened, and maybe we can help."

That made me laugh. Like they could get me back into the Underground or take care of W5, or give me money for food every day.

"Why did you run away from home?" Alisha asked.

I answered before I could stop myself. "What home are you talking about? I ain't got no home."

There it was. Now they knew I was a Streeter.

"What about your house, down by the station . . . did . . . did . . . something happen to it?" Rasheed stammered.

These two were so dumb. "I don't live there," I said with disgust. "I only pretended." I stared right into Alisha's eyes. "I don't have a home. I live on the streets. I always have, even when you met me."

Alisha gasped and put a hand across her mouth. Rasheed stood still like a statue.

He was the first to speak again. "Did you get in a fight?" he asked, pointing to my face. "And what happened to your clothes . . . like . . . are you okay?"

I could only imagine what I looked like, with a swollen eye, and ripped pants, and blood on me, and all dirty. Actually, Stink Bomb was a good name for me. I'd slept in garbage, I smelled like garbage, and I looked like garbage — and I felt like garbage too.

"Let's go in the house, Jonathon," Alisha said. Her eyes weren't wet anymore. "I bet you need something to eat. Dad and Mom are home and they'll know what to do. You can't live on the streets. That's . . . impossible. Come in, and at least eat something."

The mention of her parents got my attention. "Bad idea — real bad. Forget that." I gripped the sleeping bag tight. "I lost my sleeping bag, and I need this one. Like I said, I'll give it back when I can."

I took a deep breath and got ready to charge.

"I told you guys to hurry up. What's taking so long?"

Rasheed's father walked into the garage.

"Jonathon?"

I was done. I'd never smash past Rasheed *and* his dad. Once they found out that I'd stolen their sleeping bag, and the skates, I'd be arrested for sure.

I closed my eyes and prayed my mom wasn't watching.

Chapter 27

I tipped the bowl to get the last bit of soup. I hadn't had soup in ages, since my mom was healthy, which right now seemed like a million years ago, and it warmed my entire body all the way to my toes. This was my third bowl, and that's after I had two peanut butter sandwiches. I know I looked like a pig, but it all tasted so good I couldn't stop myself. The best part was the milk. I'd forgotten what it tasted like, and they kept filling my glass.

Honestly, I could have had another bowl of soup easy.

"My goodness, you certainly had a hunger," Cynthia said.

I'd barely looked up from my bowl the entire time. Now, with all four of them staring at me from across the table, I had to say something.

"Sorry. I had some Chinese buns yesterday. I guess I was sorta hungry, walking around last night . . . looking for a place to sleep . . . and for some reason I'm . . . I guess I'm hungry is all. I feel better; and thanks for the food."

Cynthia's eyes grew all sad. She looked a lot like Alisha.

Rick cleared his throat. "Jonathon, how can we help you?" he said.

They were always asking strange questions. "Well . . . I guess . . . you could just . . ." I was about to ask them to let me go, but I knew there was no chance, not after what I'd done. "I don't need anything," I said real quiet. "You can call the police now."

Cynthia put her hand on my arm. "Why would we call the police, dear?"

It freaked me out when she said "dear" because that's what my mom used to call me. I got this big lump in my throat and I had trouble talking.

"Jonathon, please tell us why you were in our garage, and what happened to your eye?" Cynthia asked softly.

Everyone got real quiet after that, waiting for me to answer — so that's what I did. I think I talked for hours — well, a long time anyway. I told them about my mom, and Ron taking off. I told them all about the Underground, and Rigger, and Lewis, and everyone, and W5, and Will, Rose and J.J., and getting jacked. I even told them about stealing the skates.

"So you were just skating at the arena every day when I saw you?" Rasheed said.

"I didn't have anything else to do," I said.

"Unbelievable," Rick said when I'd done talking. "I did have a feeling you weren't being completely honest with us, and I could tell by your clothes that obviously there were money problems. But I never suspected . . . It's the most incredible story I've ever heard."

"You may as well finish the rest of the soup," Cynthia said. "There's not much left anyway." She poured it into my bowl.

"Shouldn't we get some ice for his eye?" Alisha asked.

"Good idea, Ali," Rasheed said. "I'll get it."

Alisha sat beside me as I finished the soup and then put the ice on my eye. I didn't see the point, but Rasheed went to all this trouble to get it and smash it up and put it in a plastic bag. It stung at first, and then it felt kind of good. We had one of those quiet moments as everyone sat around the table. They'd been so nice to me, and obviously weren't going to call the police right away, and had fed me. Alisha looked so sad and her eyes were so big. There was one thing I had to say.

"I did something else," I began, "something kinda bad . . . to you." I took a deep breath and said in a whisper, "I stole a sleeping bag out of your van after the first practice."

"That's okay," Alisha said. "We understand. You needed it more than us, anyway."

"And we don't go camping until the summer, so it's no big deal," Rasheed said.

I looked over at Rick. "But I lost the sleeping bag," I continued. "These two drunks stole it from me last night. I don't think I can get it back." I told them what happened, and then Rasheed and his dad couldn't help laughing when I finished. It *was* kind of funny, I guess.

Alisha got real angry, though. "It's not funny!" she snapped at her dad and brother. "It's wrong that we can't take care of people and they have to live on the street; and Jonathon's a kid and he shouldn't have to . . . fight every day just to eat."

"Meet Saint Alisha," Rasheed said to me. "She's going to save the world — works with the school breakfast program every morning and volunteers at a women's shelter."

"You're so selfish, Rasheed."

Rick held his hands up. "That's enough, you two. Alisha's right, though. This is not really funny, although I confess when I think of those drunk guys all tangled up in that ugly old sleeping bag . . ."

He and Rasheed broke up again, and then Alisha began to giggle along with the rest of us.

"Quiet down, the lot of you," Cynthia said, but in a nice way. "Jonathon, we don't know exactly how, but we want to help you if you'll let us. Right, Rick?"

Rick nodded seriously.

"I imagine trusting people is not all that easy for you after all you've been through," she said. "We can't make too many promises, other than I promise you will not spend one more night sleeping on the streets. We also promise not to call the police. I do have to call some people I know who understand how to take care of kids who don't have a home to live in, and these people work for the government. Is that okay?"

I knew what government people meant. Once they heard about the electronics store and the skates and the sleeping bag, I'd end up in juvie, for sure. She had promised not to call the police, though, and if I played along I could get some more food, and sneak off when I got the chance. And I knew where the sleeping bags were.

"So is that okay?" she repeated.

"Sure. Thanks. That's real nice of you."

They all smiled after I said that.

Chapter 28

The second I heard the door close I poked my head out the bedroom door. There was some family thing going on, a reception for Cynthia's cousin who was getting married, or something like that. Rick told me they'd be back real quick. "Just have to put in an appearance," he'd said.

Well, that would give me plenty of time. The more I thought about it the more ridiculous it sounded; like I was going to wait around for Rasheed's mom to call the government. Maybe she'd get money for turning me in. Why help me in the first place? And why go on so much about trusting people — as if that wasn't suspicious? That's exactly what I'd tell someone before I double-crossed them. No one ever helped me.

I'd miss that bed, though. I couldn't believe how soft it was. What a sleep. I still couldn't believe how long I slept. It was dark outside, which meant I must have slept most of the day. Finally, my head felt clear and my headache was gone, and I could see out of my eye again. I guess that ice thing really does work.

I went downstairs to the kitchen and opened the fridge. I had to step back to take it all in. I couldn't remember when I'd seen so much food in one place, other than a supermarket: fruit, milk, cheese, yogurt, veggies, chicken, containers with leftovers, jars, drinks. I decided on the chicken, the cheese and the yogurt. I looked around for a plastic bag to carry it all.

"The plates are in the cabinet to the right of the sink, and the cutlery is underneath the top drawer."

I almost dropped the food, and I swear my heart did a cartwheel in my chest. Alisha was reading a book at the table. She smiled and pointed at the cabinets. Too stunned to think, I pulled a plate down, grabbed a spoon and some salt, although I have no idea why I needed salt, and sat down with her.

"Do you feel better, after your nap, I mean?"

I nodded and took a bite out of the chicken.

"Your eye sure looks better after icing it, although it's still kind of black and blue." She laughed a bit. "Chicken and yogurt is an interesting combination. Is that a particular favourite of yours?"

"Not sure. It's okay, I guess."

"I've been thinking about your life. That W5 must be a sad person, acting tough like that all the time and using violence. I bet he's just insecure and scared."

W5 sure didn't seem scared to me, but I didn't want to disagree with her. Best to change the subject. I asked the first question that popped into my head. "So what are you reading?"

I can be so lame.

"It's a great book — *The Catcher in the Rye*. I'm reading it again. I bet you'd love it. I'll lend it to you when I'm done."

"That would be . . . great. Sounds interesting."

She giggled again. "I didn't tell you what it was about yet."

I felt myself blush. "Oh, yeah. Well, I trust you."

"Do you?" Her eyes opened wide.

And I was about to steal from her — or at least from her family.

This was torture. I needed that sleeping bag, and yet I swear I could hear my mom talking to me. She wouldn't be happy if she knew what I was planning.

"I guess I do." That stupid lump in my throat was back. It was like I couldn't lie to her, not with Alisha looking at me so big-eyed and treating me fair. In a whisper I said, "Do you trust *me*?"

Her head jerked up. "Why wouldn't I?"

"'Cause I'm a criminal . . . I stole stuff, lots of it, and from you, and your family, and I lie all the time . . . and I . . . I was going to steal this food and I was going to steal a sleeping bag and run away to the park."

She'd hate me for sure. I didn't really know why I told her, only it felt good and somehow I knew my mom would be proud of me for saying it.

"You're no criminal. You had to steal to survive. You have to eat and get shelter, and stay warm." She sounded so certain. "Jonathon, you have to forgive yourself and start new. You need a fresh start. So repeat after me, 'I'm a good person.'"

I rolled my eyes.

"Say it," she ordered.

"This is dumb."

"It is not. Just say it like you mean it."

I paused — and the words stuck on the tip of my tongue, like really stuck, as if I couldn't get them out no matter how hard I tried.

"I can say it for you. I think you're a good person. I do. I thought that from the minute I met you."

It was the nicest thing anyone had ever said to me.

The back door opened and Rasheed walked in.

"I thought you guys were out?" I said.

Rasheed waved his hand. "Mom and Dad wanted us to stay with you. They're only going for a bit. Should we watch a movie?" He held a couple of DVDs in his hand.

"Sure," Alisha said. "We can watch downstairs, Jonathon."

I followed them to the basement. On the stairs, Rasheed turned around. "I spoke to Lou while you were sleeping — you can really sleep, dude, by the way. I bet you were out for like twelve hours. Anyway, guess what?"

I shook my head.

"All the guys want you to come back. We got a play-off game tomorrow against the Red Wings. We got smoked the first two games and if we lose again we're out. With you, we can at least make them work for it. So are you up for it?"

"I don't know. I mean, I don't think it's a good idea . . ."

It would be totally embarrassing. I couldn't go into a dressing room with a bunch of guys that called me Stink Bomb. I just couldn't. This was too much. And then I started to wonder if all of this was just crazy. These were Reggies, and here I was living with them and eating their food and trusting that they wouldn't turn me in. I wished I knew what to do. But I had no one to ask.

Rasheed laughed and pushed me on the shoulder. "All the guys understand what happened, and it's okay. Trust me. We all want you back on the team, and the coaches too."

"Even Malcolm?"

"Maybe if you pass the puck a bit more," he joked.

We both laughed at that.

"I guess Peter and Derrick aren't much worse than those two drunk guys," I joked.

"And they definitely ain't no W5," Rasheed added.

That was the truth. "How about I think it over. Maybe. I still feel kinda weird about it."

"The hockey's not so important. But you have to promise to stay and let us help you," Alisha cut in, her eyes so wide they seemed to go from ear to ear.

This was the hardest decision I'd ever had to make. I knew life on the streets could be hard — and W5 and Scrunchy Face were out there, not to mention Will. How long could I hide from them? Only I didn't know Rasheed and his family, not really. Why would they help someone like me, someone who stole their stuff and was about to do it again? I missed hockey though, more than anything except for my mom.

And there was that bed. Maybe staying and playing hockey were the smart things to do?

Chapter 29

Rasheed held the door for me. "Let's kick some Red Wing butt."

All the way over, he kept telling me everything was going to be okay. Was it really? If I heard one "Stink Bomb" comment I was out of there.

A huge smile crossed Lou's face when he saw me in the arena lobby. "Tremendous. Truly. Great to see you, Jonny." He dropped a hockey bag at my feet. "I see you've brought your magic skates." I took the skates from my shoulder and dropped them into the bag. I could have done without all the attention; I just wanted to go to the dressing room. The coaches weren't through with me yet, though.

The coaches came over, and Lou put a hand on my shoulder. "We're glad to see you back. We want to forget about the past and start over. Okay? Does that work for you?"

I mumbled, "Sure." I wasn't so sure that was really true. How could anyone forget what I said? I sure hadn't forgotten anything.

Malcolm patted me on the back. "You and I have had our differences, haven't we? But I want to put that in the past, too."

He held out his hand. I felt goofy but we shook.

"You've got a lot of talent," Malcolm continued, "and man can you skate. I've been on you to pass, and I want you to think about something before the game. Good players score goals; great players help teammates score too. And I think you can be a great player."

"I'll try, Malcolm."

"That's all we want," he said.

Lou was nodding the whole time, and he put my hockey bag on my shoulder. "Go get changed. We're in Room 4. We'll be there in fifteen minutes to talk to you guys."

I was more than happy to end the conversation. That was embarrassing. It almost made me want to drop the bag and run out of the arena. I wondered if Malcolm was being serious about me being a great player, and I got the part about passing more. I know I sometimes carry the puck too much. I promised myself to really try this game. No more Mr. Puck Hog.

I stopped in front of Room 4, and suddenly a wave of fear washed over me. I would rather have faced W5 at that moment, I was so terrified. It wasn't like they were going to pound me. But they knew my secret, that I'd been a street kid, eating out of garbage cans and hawking for money, that I had stolen stuff, and that I didn't have parents or a home. Even worse, I was still going to be Stink Bomb no matter how clean I was now.

I know kids. Like me, they wouldn't forget. I stood there, literally unable to move. I wanted to leave; and I wanted to play.

"Hurry up, Jonny," I heard Lou call out.

I took a deep breath and I pushed the door open and went inside. All talking ended in an instant. Rasheed moved his bag over and pointed next to him. I leaned my stick against the wall, and with my eyes glued to the floor, accepted his offer.

A few guys at the far end started talking, but too quiet for me to hear.

I kept getting dressed, as the guys started talking again, only still kind of quietly.

"Do you need some sock tape?" Rasheed asked me once I got to putting on my skates.

I had never used it before because it cost too much. Whenever the guys asked I said it bugged me and slowed me down. The truth was sometimes my shin pads were twisted to the side and I fell right on my knee. I was always jealous of how the guys had sock tape — and it bugged me so much that they wasted it all the time.

"I could use a bit, I guess," I said.

He tossed a roll to me. "Keep it," he said. "I got lots."

Collin leaned over. In a quiet voice, he said, "Jonathon, I gotta ask you. What was the deal with that W5 guy? Is that really his name? And did you really hit him where it counts?"

"That was Scrunchy Face," Rasheed corrected.

"I thought it was Rigger," Jacob threw in.

"Scrunchy Face was the guy I hit at the TV station," I said.

All of a sudden the questions came pouring in.

"Where is this Underground place?" Derrick asked.

"What's the Underground?" Andrew said.

"That's where he lived all this time," someone answered.

"Hey, is it true about those drunk guys fighting over Rasheed's sleeping bag?" Peter said.

"Well, the drunks, they sleep on the vent, and there were two of them . . . Yeah, it's true; and the Underground, well, it's downtown."

"How do you sleep on a vent?" Andrew said, looking confused.

"I've been all over downtown and I never saw an underground," Jacob said.

"It's a secret place — that's the point," Collin said.

Rasheed came to my rescue. "Hey, guys. Let's give Jonathon a chance to get ready. We can hammer him with questions after we win."

I shot him a grateful look and began to tie my skates. The guys began talking about the Red Wings. They'd finished first and had only lost three games all year. This was the third game of the series. The Red Wings had won the first two, and it was a must-win for us or we'd be out.

I finished with my skates as the coaches came in.

"You ready for this one?" Rasheed asked me.

I was still freaked by even being here. I wasn't really thinking about the game at all. All I could manage was a nod.

"I bet Jonathon is gonna get a hat trick. This is our game, Rangers!" he yelled.

I looked at him in shock. He began chanting, "Rangers! Ran-gers! Ran-gers!"

The other guys joined in, and then the coaches — and then guess who?

I had to. This was my team.

Chapter 30

You would not believe the difference a little food and sleep can make. Three minutes left in the third period, and I felt great, totally charged and hardly tired at all. Usually, the end of the game was torture, my stomach and head aching like crazy. I didn't feel too good about the score: 5–3 for the Red Wings. Somehow or other, even with passing the puck like mad, I had almost made good on Rasheed's bet and had scored two goals. Rasheed got the third off my pass from behind the net, which made me feel good, and Malcolm made a fuss over me on the bench.

It didn't help our chances that Jacob got a tripping penalty. Even if the Red Wings didn't score on the power play, there wouldn't be enough time to tie it up. Rasheed and Derrick were out for the kill.

"Take him, Rasheed," Lou yelled, as a Red Wing cut toward the outside in the neutral zone.

"You got him, Rasheed," I said. No one heard me, but it was funny how good it felt to say it. I don't think I'd ever cheered on the guys before.

Rasheed moved to his right and swung his stick at the puck. A huge groan went up from the Rangers' parents. His stick had caught the opposing player's blade and the player's feet went out from under him.

"He tripped over the red line, ref."

"Barely touched him."

"Why don't you give the Red Wings the game?"

I thought Rasheed had tripped him. But Lou went ballistic. It was the first time I'd seen him really lose his temper.

"Ref, you're killing the game. He falls and we get a penalty with three minutes left. Please!"

The ref barely looked over. I could tell Rasheed felt real bad about the penalty. That was definitely the game — and the season. Malcolm hopped up on the bench and huddled up with Lou, and then he came over and leaned down next to me.

"Here's the deal," Malcolm said. "We need to kill this two-man disadvantage off, and hope we can pull our goalie and tie it up. Do you think you have the wind to do that?"

He wouldn't have asked if he knew how I usually felt at the end of a game without having eaten all day.

"I feel great, coach," I said.

"Then get out there and keep the puck out of our net."

He whacked my helmet, which kind of hurt, but I didn't mind because I figured he meant it friendly.

"Go for it," Lou said.

"Your puck, Jonathon," a parent cheered.

I shuffled to the door and stepped onto the ice. Derrick saw me and came off, slapping my shin pads as we passed. "Keep us in the game," he said.

I skated over to the faceoff circle. I needed to get that puck and take some time off the penalty. That wouldn't be easy with a five-on-three, and the faceoff just outside our blue line. I hunched over the dot as the ref held the puck out.

That Matthew kid who played with me at the outdoor rink was the other centre.

"Jonathon, pull it back and I'll send it down the ice," Peter said.

The puck dropped, and Matthew tried to knock my stick away, only I had it in a reverse grip and snaked the puck back to Peter before Matthew had a chance to mess me up. Peter didn't fool around. He waited until a Red Wings forechecker came close and then blasted the puck all the way down. I couldn't believe it. He had actually done it. The puck caromed around the wall and up the side to the Red Wings' right winger, who played it back behind his net to a defenceman.

Matthew circled behind and took the puck, with the defenceman following in support. I let him get up some speed before swerving over at the blue line. He tried to power through me. Usually, I don't do much hitting, on account of being so small. Something got into me and I lowered my shoulder and threw myself into his chest. I knocked him right off his feet.

The puck slithered behind him, and the Red Wings' left winger raced after it. A second before he got it I poke-checked the puck to the side, jumped around him, and got control. Collin was too close for a pass, and the Red Wings' right winger had Peter covered. This time I had to keep it. I was strolling along the side wall, in no hurry because I wanted to kill the clock, when I heard the sound of skates charging at me. A quick glance told me it was Matthew. The guy could skate, so I picked up the pace and cut hard into the middle of the ice, about a foot outside their blue line. Then the Red Wings' right winger came at me and I had to think fast.

I couldn't go into their end, so I turned back to ours, with both Red Wings forwards hard after me. I guess my change of direction fooled Collin and Peter, and they were too close for a pass. I had to hold onto it. I hoped Malcolm wouldn't be too mad, but I thought I'd made the right choice. Anyway, I ended up all the way back in our end and eventually behind the net.

"Don't charge him," Matthew ordered, as he stopped in the slot. The two wingers camped out on the flanks, and their defencemen took the blue line. Collin and Peter came back too, but with all those players in our zone a pass would be real tough. I had to do this alone, and if I gave up the puck, they'd probably score.

A flurry of memories came into my head as I stood behind the net. A bizarre time to daydream, I admit, only I couldn't stop it. I remembered playing at the out-door rink, all those imaginary games, pretending to score the overtime goal to win the Stanley Cup, being so cold but still not caring because any hockey was better than hawking with J.J. or Will or Rose. I remembered the sound of my blades cutting into the ice, and the snap of the puck off my stick. Best of all I remembered how safe I felt when I played, no one after me, doing what I wanted. And at that moment I felt happy. Then I thought about my mom, and how happy she'd be to see me right now, and to know I wasn't hungry or cold.

I was going to kill this penalty for my teammates.

Matthew made the first move, darting to the right, and then the left winger charged from the other side. I took two strides to my right, slipped the puck between the left winger's skates, and cut forward into the slot. The right winger held out with his stick, which forced me to stickhandle to my left and just out of his reach. The right defenceman decided to stand his ground. A flick off the boards and I was past him. All that was left was a foot race with the left D, and by the blue line I was in alone. I couldn't believe it. I'd beaten five guys.

The goalie came out, slowly backing up into his crease. I wasn't going to let him spoil the moment. I'd spent hours shooting at an empty net counting how many times I could hit the post and bounce it in. At the hash marks I faked a deke and let it fly to the stick side. He was totally fooled, and I didn't even need the post. The puck plunked into the net. I'd done what Rasheed had said I would do — scored a hat trick.

Even better, we were only down by a goal and we had 1:30 left on the clock — still time to tie it up.

Peter and Collin were all over me as I skated to the bench.

"Hall-of-fame moment," Collin said, over and over.

"That was fun to watch," Peter said, slapping me on the helmet.

Did that mean he thought I hogged the puck? Peter sounded happy enough, but I was nervous. Lou leaned over the boards.

"Now that's what I call penalty killing. In ten seconds Jacob gets out, and Rasheed's out in thirty after that. Give me Derrick out there . . ." He stopped and turned to me. "Wait a sec. Jonny, how do you feel?"

I felt every kid's eyes blazing into me. Before I quit the team I'd have said I felt fine even if I was tired. And even after that shift I felt good. I could easily have kept playing, but Derrick was leaning over the bench. He really wanted to get out there.

"I could use a rest, coach," I said.

Lou nodded. "Get out there, Derrick. Jonathon will go on when we pull Andrew."

I had a feeling that wasn't the smartest thing to do if we wanted to win, but it was the smartest thing for the team because everyone cheered Derrick on and they were all happy and made a fuss over the goal.

Derrick lost the draw at centre and the Red Wings stormed our net. Jacob got on and joined the kill, but Matthew got a pass in the slot and wired a shot into the top corner just as Rasheed stepped out of the box. We were two down and only a minute to go. I flopped down on the bench. We were so close, and now we were going to lose.

"Jonathon, get ready to go on for Andrew."

"What?"

Jacob pulled me to my feet. Andrew was pounding his way to the bench.

"Get on — we're pulling the goalie!" Jacob yelled in my ear, and he practically threw me over the boards. Lou was yelling at Rasheed to get it in deep, and Malcolm was at the other end of the bench. "Go, Rangers, go!" he shrieked. The Rangers' parents had completely lost it also and they were all chanting, "Rangers! Ran-gers!" I landed on the ice and tore after the puck. Maybe we could get a couple of quick goals and force another game. This season wasn't over. Think of me half-starving in Rasheed's garage and now I was playing hockey and had never felt better. Miracles do happen.

The puck came back to Collin and he drilled it on the net. An insane scramble developed in front, Rasheed whacking at it by the side of the net, and he eventually sent the puck spinning to the corner. I was on it and passed back to Collin who one-timed it, only it hit someone and the puck bounced back to me in the corner. I figured Collin had a wicked shot so I passed it right back to him. This time he went far side and the goalie kicked out his pad, sending the puck spinning to Derrick against the boards. He battled for it and was able to cycle it down low to Rasheed who surprised everyone by whistling it all the way along the wall to Collin.

This time he stopped it and wound up. I spotted a lane to the net and went for it just as the shot came in. A Red Wings winger tried to slow me down but I was like a madman. Derrick was pounding with a defence-man on the other side and Jacob, who was usually a wimp, was bulling his way to the net.

The puck whistled past me and hit the goalie in the chest. He dropped to the butterfly to try and freeze the puck, only Jacob dove and knocked it free. It dribbled toward me and for a second I thought I could jam it in the short side but a defenceman dropped to his knees and I had nothing to shoot at.

"Jonathon. Back!"

That sounded like Peter. I whirled with the puck on my forehand and there he was all by himself at the top of the circle. Great players help their teammates score — that's what Malcolm said — so I slid the puck back, not too hard, so he wouldn't miss. And he didn't. He reared back and blasted it over the goalie's shoulder and into the net. Peter actually scored — his first goal since I'd joined the team. Another miracle.

We all huddled to celebrate. Everyone was scream ing and high-fiving. It was totally mental. I snuck a peek at the clock — twenty seconds. There was still time. We lined up, and Derrick won the draw. Peter passed to Rasheed who one-timed it into their end. I'd never skat-ed so hard in my entire life. The Red Wings defenceman had it on his forehand. I was two metres away. If I could just knock it away we had a chance.

But the defenceman had other ideas. He wristed the puck way high. It flew over everyone and bounced at the red line and dribbled toward our net.

Collin raced back for it, but the Red Wings

forecheckers were all over him, and then the buzzer sounded to end the game. I almost couldn't understand. We'd lost; and the series was over; and so was the season.

No more miracles.

Next thing I felt an arm around my neck.

"Nice game, Jonathon," Rasheed said.

He didn't look happy, but he didn't look like he was going to cry, either.

"Unbelievable pass," Peter said to me. "Tough one. We just ran out of time. We could have beaten these guys."

"Next year for sure," Collin said, tapping everyone's shin pads with his stick. "We keep this team together, we can do it."

I wondered if that included me.

Chapter 31

I waited for Rasheed and Collin to pile out of the van.

"You guys head in," Rick told them. "Give me a sec with Jonathon."

"Sure, Rick," Collin said, and they went into Johnny's. I could see a few of the other Rangers through the window, already in there.

Rick turned around in his chair to face me. "You can head on in also," he said to Alisha.

She shook her head. "I'll wait."

"I need to speak to Jonathon in private, Alisha."

"I'm okay," she said, arms crossed. "Besides, I don't want to go in with a bunch of dumb boys."

"Alisha, please!"

"I don't mind," I jumped in. I really didn't. I liked the idea of her staying.

"Well, this affects her too, so why not? Jonathon, Cynthia met with a woman from Child and Family Services — think of her as a social worker."

My throat went dry suddenly.

"A few options were discussed. Certainly, you need

a safe and secure environment in which to grow up, and you need to go back to school. We also believe that playing hockey is important, not only because you're a great player, but also because it gives you a chance to meet other boys and keep fit.

"Cynthia reviewed some possible foster homes. Some were too far from the city, others had older kids, and I think one had little ones."

I could tell he was beating around the bush. He didn't want to tell me. I looked over at Alisha. I was really going to miss her — and Rasheed — and all the Rangers.

"Anyway, to get right to it, Cynthia and I want you to give this some thought: we believe that the best place for you right now is with us. We have the extra bedroom, and you and Rasheed and Alisha seem to get along well, and we would like to do it. And, well, what I mean is, we want to be your foster parents — that is, if you are comfortable with the idea."

My brain had trouble taking it in. What did he want with me? How was this possible? I mean — what exactly was he getting at? Rick was obviously waiting for me to say something.

"Please say yes, Jonathon," Alisha said. "It's perfect. Why go somewhere else when you belong right here?"

I wanted to talk, only I couldn't. It was as if the words wouldn't hop over my teeth, and then if you can believe it a few tears leaked out of my eyes. I knew I was acting dumb, and I was lucky Rasheed and Collin weren't here. I wiped them away double quick with my sleeve, although actually it was Rasheed's since he lent me this shirt.

The silence was getting real awkward. Alisha was looking at me with those big eyes, and Rick just sat there the way adults do when they want you to talk to them, and be honest, and all that kind of emotional Reggie stuff. That made me think. When did I stop being a Reggie? And why was I still thinking like an Undergrounder?

All the street kids told me you couldn't trust a Reggie, especially Lewis. Maybe that was true about some of them. But it couldn't be true about all of them. I knew now that Lewis was wrong about a lot of things, and maybe that included Reggies.

I guess I just could not believe Alisha was lying. It was impossible, or at least I didn't want to think it was possible. And I guess I really wanted to believe Rick and Cynthia were being honest too. Was this really happening? It was like every Undergrounder's dream, to have a house to live in, and food, and a bed. And Rick was offering it to me. So what was my problem?

I was going to have to give them some sort of answer.

"We could do it for a few days . . . or a week . . . whatever. I don't mind, I guess . . . until it's a problem . . . or you find somewhere else . . ."

All of a sudden I lost my train of thought. I was getting lamer by the second.

Rick had this weird smile on his face, not a laughing smile but one that seemed serious. It was weird and nice at the same time. Alisha had the same smile. I had no idea how my face looked — probably goofy.

"Cynthia thought it would be best if we all agreed that you would stay with us for six months," Rick said. "She feels, as I do, that it would be better for you to stay in one place, in our home, for a solid chunk of time. If things don't work out, we can look at other options, other places to stay. It's up to you. But I would really like you to say yes."

"Jonathon!" Alisha pleaded. "This is silly. Could you just say yes so we can eat?"

Six months? It wasn't that long really. I could always leave if I wanted. He said there were other places. And I would really have trouble saying goodbye to that bed . . .

I decided not to make a big deal of it. "If you think it's a good idea, I guess I will. Thanks, I guess. I mean, it's nice of you . . . you don't have to . . . but if you want to, then . . . Okay. I'll try it."

Rick nodded. "I'll take that as a yes. Welcome to our home. Now let's eat."

We all got out and went into Johnny's.

"Do you want the usual?" Rick asked me.

He really was in a weird mood because I had only been here once, so how could I have a usual? But since he was being so nice about the foster parent thing I said, "Sure."

"Yo, Jonathon, come on over." Collin was standing at a table waving at me. He was with Rasheed, Derrick, Jacob and Peter.

"Go ahead," Alisha said. "I'll wait with my dad."

I went over and sat next to Derrick.

"We were talking about next year," Collin said. "You're going to play with us, right?" he asked me.

Rick had said he wanted me to play hockey; he could only have meant with the Rangers. "I'd like to — if there's a spot."

They roared so loud I thought the owner would kick us out. "We'll see if we can squeeze you into the lineup," Collin said.

"Have you figured out where you're going to stay?" Derrick asked suddenly, and all the boys stopped laughing.

I felt my face get all hot. "I think I might be going to stay with Rasheed, I mean, with Rasheed's family."

"Did you give it the okay?" Rasheed asked me.

I nodded.

"How awesome is that?" Rasheed said. "Jonathon is going to stay with us. It'll be like having the brother I've always wanted, and I won't have to put up with an irritating sister by myself."

"She's not irritating," I began.

They made a big deal about that and whooped it up and joked about me and Alisha beating up on Rasheed.

The guys started to talk about the season, and Rasheed told the story of playing shinny with me that first time, and how he got the idea of asking me to join the Rangers. Then they made me tell the story about the drunks and the sleeping bag, and everyone laughed their heads off. Reggies sure think that story is funny.

Lou and Rick carried over a couple of trays and laid them on our table.

"Go for it, animals," Lou said.

The smell of the food hit me, and for the first time in ages I didn't get dizzy and my mouth didn't start watering like a river. I was hungry, sure — but not like before. I let the others go first and then grabbed my burger.

"This is yours too," Rasheed said, giving me another one. "Gotta do the double double."

I tore into the first burger. We all got quiet as we started eating. I guess I wasn't the only hungry kid. I munched away, looking out the window to watch the snow fall. It was getting kind of heavy, almost like a storm. I would sure hate to be outside tonight.

I raised my eyes to the ceiling and imagined my mom looking down.

I'm okay, Mom, I thought. I think things will be better now.

About the Author

David Skuy spent most of his childhood playing one sport or another — hockey, soccer, football, rugby. When he wasn't playing sports, he was reading books about them. Now he is a writer and lawyer who lives in Toronto, Ontario, with his wife and two kids. He still plays hockey once a week and remains a diehard Maple Leafs fan.

He began writing books for young readers to try to capture the competition, the challenges, the friendships and the rivalries that make sports so much fun.

Other books by David Skuy:

The Game Time series
Off the Crossbar
Rebel Power Play
Making the Cut